TRIPPING

OVER

THE OCEAN

Tripping Over the Ocean

Anne Millen

ISBN: 978-0-9941648-2-7
ISBN: 0994164823

Published by Pumicestone Publishing
Banksia Beach
Queensland 4507
Australia

Photographs by Anne Millen
Contact: **annemillenauthor@gmail.com**

Cover art work:
Ketch Under Sail © by Gaynor Mulholland 2016

Gaynor Mulholland

Gaynor Mulholland is a Whanganui-based artist who says that she paints to create visual delight for herself and others. Having lived most of her life in large chaotic cities, she values the space and stillness of New Zealand. Through her representational oil and water colour paintings, she tries to bring that into her world, and, she hopes, into yours.

Contact:

gaynormulholland@gmail.com

Acknowledgements

More than a few people have helped me with this novel. Gaynor Mulholland, my talented friend in Whanganui, painted Ketch Under Sail for the front cover—a cover that surpassed my dreams, and of which I very much hope my story is worthy.

These three helped with my text: Sandi Ellis who, early on, insisted I continue and gave me excellent advice; Maurie Robertson, who helped enormously on sailing matters, even rescues at sea, and Richard Woodd, who used his journalistic expertise to advise on various points of style and to detect inconsistencies and errors. To all three I owe thanks for their encouragement.

Jane Northcote was generous indeed with her support, an inspiring work space, and help with publicity and networking. Thank you, Jane!

I am grateful to Linda Read, in Brisbane, who kindly edited my manuscript and was as kind as an editor can be, and to Julia Millen who re-edited it after all my changes. I am grateful, too, to Donna Munro who helped me with the publishing process, and the many people who helped in myriad ways to get this book to print. It has suffered a few years delay but no doubt benefitted from that.

Chapter One

Aria began whittling a plan while the wind rose steadily to thirty knots. She knew anyone going to sea needs a good solid plan, one that includes the possibility of changing the whole thing.

Trinkitat heeled more and more. Aria put her thoughts aside and squeezed her watering eyes into a tight squint. The south-westerly wind bit her face and brilliant light glanced up from the waves, but she kept her attention on the channel ahead. *Trinkitat* tore on, hard on a beam reach, spray flying high over the bow each time she struck a wave. The decks were drenched and water gushed from the scuppers. Down past Motutapu Island with Motuihe to port, she held on towards Brown's Island, then moved gradually into the middle of the Motukorea channel. Aria took her hand from the tiller and clawed a strand of wet hair from her face to the hood of her oilskin.

The Auckland harbour opened up while the sun was still high. Aria flicked her narrowed eyes over the straining sails and sheets and back to the channel. Her heart sang, *I can do it, I can do it alone*! She did not let herself smile—her lips were so dry and cold she was afraid they might split. To starboard, black Rangitoto reared its jagged rocks, making her want to cling to the channel.

A big merchant vessel, loaded and heavy in the water, was making way slowly out of the harbour in the main shipping lanes. It was still a long way off, accompanied by tugs. Aria would reach the main channel and then tack back to the eastern side of it. She watched the ship's bearing. When she had changed tack, *Trinkitat* would pass in front of it. She knew that if she did it clean and fast while the behemoth was still well up-channel, she would be quite safe.

The first crossing had been quick, because of the bend in the channel. She knew she could sail some way beyond the marked waterway, watching the depth sounder, but she could not take much time on the next tack—who knew when the ship might pile on steam? *Trinkitat* and the ship should pass port to port if they were both in the channel, but she should be across and out of it well before the big vessel passed her. Aria watched and waited, her jubilation bubbling up amid her caution. The wind came round to the west a few points. She checked the bearing of the ship again.

Through motionless lips, Aria sang a few lines of *Show Me the Way*, the heat of her breath comforting her stinging lips. Her father and Carlotta, his crew, used to sing that. Carlotta was the Styx fan; he had not really known the words but that had not stopped him joining in, gloriously off-key, when he was sailing and happy. Aria started on another, *Come Sail Away*, watched the depth sounder, the sails, and the ship's bearing and thought about sailing with her dad …

…Now! Ready for the whack of the mainsail coming across, not far but uncontrolled, she threw the tiller over, released the starboard jib sheet carefully and hauled the port sheet in with her left hand. Her right hand held the smooth dark wood of the tiller. The winch whirred and slowed as she brought it in hard, one foot braced against the cockpit seat. She drew in the main and *Trinkitat* came up a bit more. She had left only the last reef out.

Aria's nose was running, and her eyes watering. She sniffed hard, put the winch handle on and cranked the jib sheet in. Not a perfect tack, maybe, but she was now on a close reach. The ship was still beyond Bean Rock, but heading straight for her.

Aria kept an eye on the masthead vane. The wind was backing further. She brought the jib sheet in more and more until she was hard on the wind, straining her sails and washing her lee rail, paralleling the side of the channel. She hoped she could stay on the same tack until the ship passed her.

Aria thought of the three times she had helped her father bring their old yacht *Filly* back from the Noumea race. Occasionally, they'd had winds as strong this, with the big swell of the ocean, but *Filly* had taken it easily. Each time, they had managed to keep pretty much on one tack the whole way. They had done watch-about but Dad somehow kept an eye on things, even when he was sleeping. Now she thought how very different, how freeing it was, to single-hand.

She eyed the big ship looming up, reassessing constantly. Their courses were only slightly divergent, but she could always do a quick tack further off. The wind was now almost round to the west. She kept her course along the edge of the channel. The ship would be stories above and not far enough away for her to keep the wind once in its lee. She would probably have to let *Trinkitat* wallow and luff her sails for a few minutes.

And there it was, the messy lull in the ship's lee. Not all wind disappeared, but *Trinkitat* lost her speed, and her headsail luffed a bit. The rusting *Konglong* hogged the channel, less than two cables away, engines thundering. When the wind came back, Aria could expect a good hard slam. In the brief calm, she grabbed a rag from the pocket of her oilskin trousers and wiped her nose. She stuffed it back in as the wind struck violently again and *Trinkitat* surged forward.

A catamaran shot out past the ship's stern, bucking and flying, a huge headsail blocking the helmsman's view to starboard. They were on a collision course. Aria gasped. The hair on her arms and neck prickled. She threw the tiller over hard and flipped the sheets off. *Trinkitat* slewed round parallel to the catamaran, and they passed so close that Aria feared the tossing cat might catch her rigging. Then they were past and she roared "Idiots!" into the wind.

One man heard her and turned. She saw his mouth open. They all turned and looked. Then one slapped the helmsman's back and they all rocked with laughter, luffing their sails momentarily and slowing. Aria read *Hubbi's Darling* on the stern as they regained direction.

She grimaced. Who's amazed? she thought, I bet all that holds that thing down on the water is crates of beer. At least we're out of it unscathed.

She remembered her wry old navigation teacher, Charlie, explaining the rules for the avoidance of collision at sea. "Don't worry about the outcome if you *know* you're in the right. You can cut the other boat in half. Just make sure you know the rules and stick to them so you look good at the inquiry. You'll look even better if you turn round and rescue the survivors, pick up any bodies." There had been a collective in-breath before most of his students leaned forward, frowning, saying earnestly, "But Charlie … !"

Trinkitat had done a circle and was lying bow to the wind in irons, her sails flogging amidships. Aria checked the depth sounder, glad that *Trink* did not draw much, in spite of her first owner adding thirty centimetres to her keel. Plenty of water, though she was now well out of the channel. Aria re-sheeted her main and yankee, caught the wind and tacked back into the channel. Her rancour was gone; she knew she had done well. I can handle whatever it throws at me, she thought, and I will do a single-handed blue water passage. She allowed herself to laugh and her lips did not split.

The harbour was almost clear of yachts now; there was nothing like half a gale to send them all home. For the rest of her way up the harbour, she kept to the channel, tacking hard on the wind, grateful for few other vessels. Past the city half-obscured by spray and glare where she knew Mat, her ex-husband, would be watching for her with binoculars, she held on. By late afternoon, she dropped her sails and chugged slowly into the marina. Her nose was ice cold and streaming, her skin wind-burned, but her heart was soaring. Things had changed.

***

From her berth, Aria was glad to see her younger sister Aubrey, whom she called Bree, on the yacht club verandah. She worried about Bree; she was nine years younger than Aria and the gap seemed huge.

Her boyfriend Manny sat at a table with a few other men. She sighed. Manny was a pain, and had made something of a mess of Bree's life. As far as Aria could see, he had no real friends, just an odd, ever-changing bunch of smart-mouthed men younger than himself. Bree was generous and gave everyone the benefit of the doubt. Aria suspected Bree had covered for him a few times and thought wryly of how often, on the water, well-meaning but unskilled rescuers had to be rescued themselves. "Manny has a personality problem and that won't change," Aria had often said to her. "Don't keep wasting time on him. He's not the guy for you." But Bree hung in. That was Bree; she could love the unlovable. Perhaps she only saw his good looks. He was all brown—brown hair, brown skin, brown eyes and it was a smooth, golden, delicious brown. Bree had met him in Singapore on a school trip. He was years older than her but he had kept in touch. Then he had turned up in Auckland. She had wasted her university years on him and welcomed him back after he had vanished, unexplained, for months.

Bree could make out Aria's tall figure moving around the deck tidying up. She wondered why Aria didn't get something with more headroom. But, she thought, that's Arz; she didn't look for comfort or company. A spartan H28 was very her.

Aria took her time to do a clean-up on *Trinkitat*. She checked the bilges, coiled the sheets, bagged the jib and dragged her tatty covers over the main and mizzen. Every moment aboard, even the tidying after a trip, was delicious. Eventually, she collected the detritus of the voyage and closed up. She would come down during the week and sort *Trink* out properly. She did not bother combing her salt-laden tangled hair, and headed for the showers.

Bree still leaned on the verandah rail watching her, Manny in a huddle over the table with the others. Aria saw Bree turn to speak to him and touch his arm, but he shook her off. She turned back, accepting exclusion. Aria sighed. Bree! She went on up the path to the club's shower block.

Upstairs she found her sister. "Come and sit somewhere else. I don't think I can take a dose of these guys after the idiots I had to deal with today." She spoke softly but did not really care if any of them heard.

Bree laughed. "Sure. What idiots? Tell me about it."

Aria had put on beige and black linen and added high heels. Bree walked behind her. She thought how elegant Aria looked, apart from her wet hair. Aria always walked tall—back straight, chin drawn back, fast but with an economy and grace of movement. And only Arz could go up to Opua sailing for a week in that cramped, smelly little boat and keep her shore clothes tidy.

Aria chose a table in a corner of the bar. It was not quiet; the background music—Baby Blue and other George Baker songs—was loud enough to make everyone speak up. She laughed. "That music! We could be in the 'Naki, where they still play that stuff. Oh, Bree, that was some sail! But now I know I can handle her again; she's a cracker little yacht. That must have been a good thirty knots out there."

Bree smiled. Aria had always had to prove herself—to her, to their father, to the world. Even now he was gone, she was still doing it. She had sold his boat, kept the berth and bought an H28, roughly rigged for single-handing. She re-rigged it to make handling easier, then went out most weekends, whatever the weather, and came back tangle-haired, lip-chapped and grinning. Her blonde hair looked dark, combed straight and stuck to her head with moisture dribbling down her neck. Tomorrow morning, she would appear in chambers or in court, neat-suited and groomed, severe and unsmiling. That's Aria too, Bree thought. She got up and walked to the bar.

Lights began to twinkle across the harbour. Bree brought drinks back, the condensation wetting the menu. Aria yawned. "I haven't had a whole bunch of food or sleep. Good to be in, really."

Bree peered out at the men Manny had asked along. "I had to put those guys down as your guests, Arz. Embarrassing! They seem really dodgy to me—won't talk much while I'm around. And some of them barely speak English."

"Uhuh. Look like dope dealers to me the way they keep glancing around. Get shot of Manny and you get shot of his awful mates. Just give him the flick. Your life'll be good again." Bree gave a half smile, and Aria knew she had no intention of it. They ate grilled fish with paua fritters and chips and Aria told Bree about the near collision. "They were much too close behind the ship, dangerously close. If that thing bit into the churning water they'd have been in trouble."

Bree was murmuring, "Well, risk appeals to nutters," when a deep voice cut across her.

"Hey *Trinkitat*, you were slow. *Hubbi's Darlin'* came in just behind you but we caught a coupl'a three fish and a beer in Islington Bay. What took you?"

Aria bristled but kept chewing her tough paua fritter. He waited. She looked up at a broad tanned face with a mischievous grin. "What you did was stupid and irresponsible," she growled, "You shouldn't be out there."

"We didn't see you. And boy, that ship cut up a wake!" He had a hint of a North American accent.

Aria snorted and turned away from him.

"Hey, lighten up! Let me take you to dinner during the week, to make up for my being stoopid and irresponsible. Here's my card—call me". There was a laugh behind his voice.

"I won't."

"Then what if I say I'm sorry?"

"You'd be insincere."

"Woho, you're a hard woman! Okay, okay, chastised. Au revoir."

Aria slid the card under a beer mat without looking at it. Bree's eyes followed him to the door. "He might be a cheeky yob, Arz, but he's damn good looking." He had a strong face, honey-coloured, with long dark eyelashes and dark eyes.

"Grab him, then. He might be an improvement." They laughed. Bree kept her eyes on the door and Aria reached across for her hand to get her attention. "Seriously, Bree, I'm thinking of doing a single-handed passage. Tonga, Fiji, Port Vila, I don't know. I've done a hard week's sailing, and a really hard sail today and I had no problem. I can get a sheet in with either hand again. I don't think there is anything I can't do. Well, I still can't get full strength with my arm straight up, but I don't think it matters. And I wouldn't have to take that much time off work to do it. Preparation's probably going to be slow, because I would have to have everything perfect before ..."

"But Arz, why? Why single-hand? It's so much safer if there's two of you. Get crew."

"You know what a tight squeeze *Trink* is for two. Whoever crews would need to be a very close friend. And I've set her up for single-handing because that's the thrill for me."

Bree looked at her over her coffee cup. "A very close friend is exactly what you need, Arz."

"Oh give up, Bree. I just don't do men. Mat was about as good as they get, and I couldn't do Mat. Idiot that he is. They are all idiots one way or another. Sooner or later you realise it."

Bree laughed and gathered up her coat. "Come on, let's go home—while men are copping it not me. I suppose you need to gather your strength to slaughter an *idiot* in court tomorrow. You got stuff to pick up? I'll just tell Manny I'm going." Aria waited for her, and as they turned towards the outer door, she glimpsed the *Hubbi's Darling* skipper, sprawled in a horseshoe chair, watching her with a grin.

Chapter Two

Oscar dragged on his wetsuit, grunting with the effort. He'd had a hard game of rugby in the early afternoon and a long rake-over by their coach. Now it was late but he'd said he would go over and scrape any growth off *Pssst!*'s propeller. He knew it was not urgent but the owner had promised more jobs after this one. Up on deck, he strapped on his knife, readied and fitted his mask.

A few boats along, across the pontoon, a woman sat on her foredeck, smiling. She was whittling and must have been listening to music or remembering something pretty good. The low sun lit her pale hair with gold. Music drifted over to him from several directions, under the voices and the clink of not-yet-secured halyards. By the time the sun went down, the marina would be silent apart from the whistle of the wind, every slapping halyard pulled out to a stay; that was the sort of place it was. *Trinkitat*, the woman's yacht was called. Odd name, he thought—it's a port on the African side of the Red Sea. He wondered if the boat had come from there. It was small, but had that practical ocean-going look.

Below, he worked fast, hoping not to have to come down a second time. Using too much force on the last large barnacle, he struck his knuckles on the bronze blade. The knife flipped out of his hand. He grabbed it quickly—if it went into the sludge at the bottom of the marina, he'd never see it again.

Oscar glimpsed two small sharks before he swam powerfully up, caught the edge of the pontoon and threw himself up in one smooth movement to land in a crouch. In the next instant he was standing and saw a swirl below him.

It had been a mistake to grab the knife. His hand, cut across the palm and fingers, was a bloody mess. The cut looked superficial but was bleeding freely. He put the knife back in its holder, dribbling diluted blood on his foot and the pontoon. He closed his fist, pressing his fingers in tight across it, washed the blood off his foot and the back of his hand under the freshwater tap and jumped aboard *Pssst!* to clean up and get dry.

There was nothing much aboard. He wound some of his clothing round his hand, peeled off his wetsuit and had to free his hand to get it through the sleeve. The blood welled up again. He put the binding back around it and wrapped his towel clumsily around his waist when he heard someone knock on the hull.

"Aboard *Pssst!*"

He scrambled up the companionway. "Hi. Ahh, you're from *Trinkitat*, eh."

"Yes. I wondered … I noticed there was blood on the wharf and some sharks around the pontoon. What happened? You ok? You stood there looking stunned for a while …"

His hair was tied up and there was a streak of blood on his forehead. "Cut my hand cleaning the prop—well, stopping my knife going into the mud. I guessed there was a risk. Hence the fast exit." He grinned and held up his hand, lime green underpants wrapped round it and gripped into the palm.

Aria pulled the corners of her mouth down but her eyes were crinkled with amusement. "I can do a better dressing than that. Come over when you're ready." She walked off along the pontoon with a graceful fluency of movement.

He watched her going and laughed aloud. It would not be hard to do a better dressing. He dragged on his clothes without any undies and trotted along to her boat to knock on the cabin top. "Come aboard!" A proper first aid kit was open on the small saloon table. He sat on the settee, leaning over to keep his hand above the table and took off the wrapping. "It's nothing much, I think." He spread his fingers and a few spots of blood appeared.

Aria bent over his hand. "Can you move all your fingers? Do everything? Yes, for all that blood, it's not so deep—you haven't cut anything that matters." She was quick and efficient and ignored his flinch when she wiped the Betadine firmly across the little flaps of skin. "Might need to give your face a clean-up before anyone sees you in the street."

He spat on a clean bit of the underpants and wiped his forehead. "OK now? Don't look like I've been in a pub brawl? Thanks for the dressing. There's almost nothing on board that thing. It's very new. Well, hardly used." He pressed the adhesive firmly. "Crazy name, *Trinkitat*. You won't want to put out a mayday." He half stood to stuff the pants in his pocket and flopped back down again.

"Yes, bit long. But not as crazy as *Pssst!*. Can you imagine? Mayday mayday mayday yacht *Pssst! …* mayday *Pssst! …*"

When he laughed, his whole handsome face scrunched up, big dark eyes alight. "Yeah, well, not my boat. Some smart arse. He just hired me to do a few jobs and clean his prop. So where did you get *Trinkitat*?"

She rocked her weight onto the foot-pump to fill the kettle and wondered which of the Pacific Islands his family were from. He sounded like any Kiwi. "She was built in Whangarei. She's GRP, pretty new as H28s go—about six years old and in really good shape." She lit the stove under the kettle and carefully adjusted the flame. "She's always been a single-hander; old Hans Martinsen built her and fitted her out, somewhat basically, for solo sailing after his wife died. He reckoned a ketch is the safest and easiest to sail. They were friends of Dad's, the Martinsens—*real* sailors. They brought a little double-ender out from Denmark; sailed round the Cape of Good Hope and the bottom of Australia. It would have been pretty challenging."

Oscar whistled. "That's real! But I just meant the name."

She tipped tea leaves into her palm and threw them into a battered metal teapot. The kettle was already simmering noisily, but she moved slowly. "Oh, I named her after my childhood cat. We lived on a farm and I had a grey cat …" She had an impulse to tell him absolutely everything and stifled it. "Hans had called her *Marta M* after his wife. When I bought her, everyone said she's so small I'd pretty soon change it to martyr*dom* ..." Aria glanced round her and shrugged. "But … she's a great little yacht. She's sweet."

"Sweet, eh?" He laughed again, a deep rumble like distant thunder. "Yeah, she's sweet alright. You go out much? So many gaps on the pontoons every weekend I never noticed. That thing..." he gestured back towards *Pssst!* "… I reckon it's never moved. Don't know how it got there."

"I go out every chance I can. I had a week off recently and sailed her up to Opua. Hard blow coming up the channel. It was fantastic." Her face broke into a wide uninhibited grin. "I've decided I'll do a single-handed ocean passage. Don't know how I'll wangle that with work but …" She shrugged. "If I can't get enough time, I might be tempted to quit." She darted a quick look at him, suddenly hoping he didn't think she was just a big talker.

"Hah! You and me both. I worked in Dubai for two years—I marry banks—and now I'm back I'm pretty bored. There's no banks merging here … I dunno, just humdrum stuff with systems, new systems, better systems, going sideways into auditing. I spend my time wondering what else I can do and still eat."

"Don't look like you eat regularly now. Want a ginger biscuit?" She poured tea into mugs and gave it to him black. "Haven't got milk or sugar. Or cupcakes." That was pretty lame; she wished she could be amusing so she could hear his laugh again.

"Tea and bikkies is fine. Seems like everyone here drinks wine aboard and brings fancy catered canapés. *Pssst!* has very little of anything useful, but plenty of entertaining stuff. *Glass* glasses, trays, a fridge with ice-maker and so on."

"Who owns her?"

"Some investment guy. I met him at a bank thing. Pretty crass. He said, "Samoan huh? Betcha swim like a fish, sail a boat, climb coconut trees—all the tropical island stuff". I was wearing a suit and carrying a briefcase. But he's right, I do, even though I grew up here in Godzone."

Ah, Samoa. "Did you? Where?"

"Here in Auckland, only I wasn't here much. Mum and Dad sent me to Christ's College in Christchurch to get me away from the naughty Samoan boys. Haha, they would've been more fun."

"Parents are always afraid their children are going off the rails. Even when they're clearly not."

"Then I just carried on at Canterbury and did Computer Science and Finance. Had a shaky start; I wasted a year, pretty much, on rugby and a band and changing courses but I'd started young so it didn't matter too much." He pressed on the dressing.

"Yeah, that's how I turned out a good Samoan boy. But I spent every long holiday in Samoa with rellies—I got a lot of amazing cuzzies there." He laughed at his memories but he felt he'd told his life story in a minute flat. "Hey, thanks for fixing this." He waved his dressed hand.

Aria nodded. "You doing much boat stuff?"

"Whatever I can get. I like messing around in here—even if there's sharks. But just as likely to get eaten at work, eh." His laugh rumbled briefly. "I gotta be somewhere else soon. Thanks for the tea." He stood, head bowed to avoid the coach roof, and moved to the companionway. "You don't mind having no headroom?"

"I'm used to it, and, really, a single-hander ends up spending her time in the cockpit. Yep, see you around—bye." She followed him up and stood there, arms folded.

"I'll be down again next weekend. Maybe see you then. Maybe …"

She said nothing and he walked off, up the pontoon.

He looked back as he reached *Pssst!*. She was watching him from her dodger and gave a brief wave. He called back, "Hey, my name's Oscar!" and then felt embarrassed. Why hadn't he introduced himself properly to start with? Then he would have known her name. Ah, but she's probably a whole bunch older than me, he thought, five years at least. He shrugged and carried on up the pontoon. He'd see if he could get a few more jobs around the marina, or more on *Psssst!* anyway.

***

In her letter box, Aria found a note from Harky Paulsen, Carlotta's friend, saying he had not heard from Carlotta in a fortnight and asking her to make enquiries. Harky lived on the

Coromandel Peninsula, at Whitianga. As the seagull flew, it was not far but it was a long trip by road or sea. Harky avoided all modern communications, considered a telephone too expensive and wrote letters. "Inasmuch as I choose solitude, so do I need that which breaks it to make it more enjoyable," he wrote. Aria laughed. Very Harky. His spoken language was fortunately not so elaborate.

Harky had been born in Norway, but moved with his family from one diplomatic posting to another and went to secondary school in England. He wore a sailor's cap and doffed it to women; with men, he stood ramrod straight and shook hands. It made him seem much older than he was, a museum piece, she thought. Now he lived on a small farm near Whitianga, where he was popular in the local community but made himself invisible during the holiday influx. He whittled, too. He had sometimes given Aria a piece, and that was what had started her whittling.

She called Carlotta's number. There was no answer so she called the hospital.

"Oh, Carlotta … she's gonna be in tomorrow, weather permitting. No, never answers her phone—we're used to it. I'll tell her you called. It's Aria, isn't it? I know your voice now."

Aria wrote back to Harky saying that she had not seen Carlotta for about two weeks either but, having rung the hospital where she was expected the following day, believed all to be well and would certainly let him know if it were otherwise. His address was just RD1, Whitianga. She smiled to herself; her own written English became more formal in the face of Harky's elegant second-language version.

Carlotta's did not. When she finally heard from Carlotta, Aria had to hold the phone away from her ear. "Fanny! That boy! I could write him but what would I say? I work, I sleep, I keep my boat afloat. There's never anything different. I'll sail down there and surprise him, maybe. Just take a couple of days off. I love that trip."

There was another note, this one clearly delivered by hand. It was from Mat. "Aria, love of my life, I miss you as much as ever. Lunch or dinner one day next week? I have a short day Wednesday. Call me. Your Matiu XXX"

Mat. The bitterness of disappointment and grief swept over her again. Mat had seemed everything she wanted in a partner. He liked sailing, camping, music, dancing, had a giant sprawling family full of crazy wonderful musical people, and a good career—though after some of his more irresponsible exploits, Aria suspected he was given a little extra leeway because he was Māori, charming and the only traditionally tattooed doctor.

They had only had a few years together, but it had been a wonderful time. Mat was two years younger than her, so she had been working while he was still a student. He was in the long hard slog of his final year and internship but managed to do things with her and wrap her in love and care. What had happened?

She went out to the balcony and gazed out over the harbour. She loved this view—it was why she loved living here so much—and it had been her comfort throughout the difficulties of the past eighteen months. Now she sought its calming effect again.

When she came in, Aria sighed and dropped the little card on the kitchen bench. It was not fair. He had taken himself out of her life when she had needed him. Now he expected to walk back in after she had made other plans. She missed him too; sometimes she caught herself singing *"You left and took the stars away ..."* It had been one of her grieving songs.

Chapter Three

George Bettison looked up over his glasses and called, "Come in, Miss Stihl." He dropped his eyes to his desk, stuck a marker on the side of a page and closed the folder. "Do sit down. I'd like you to take this on. It is a complicated case, so take your time, but I have confidence that you will tease the threads out well." He showed her the folder name.

"Thank you, Mr Bettison. I'm aware of it, and already awash in the opinions of the press."

He laughed.

She took a breath, half rose and sat down again. She forced herself to look directly at his eyes. "Mr Bettison, I would like to take some leave without pay. Next April … or May, perhaps."

He pulled his glasses off. "You've just had some leave and went sailing, I hear. Next year? We'd have to see closer to the time. This case might not be over before next April. And you had three months off last year. I know that was medical— unavoidable—but it was difficult enough for the practice." He pushed his glasses up again, his voice gentler. "Er … are you anticipating another … er, health problem? I certainly hope not."

Isiah Macdonald appeared in the doorway and Bettison held up a finger to stop him. Isiah was from Espiritu Santo, educated in Port Vila and Auckland, and one of Bettison's favourite articled clerks. He added a lightness, a gentle disregard for formality to the office. He nodded and leaned against the door frame.

Aria turned back to the desk. "No, I'm fine. I want to do a single-handed ocean passage. It's the kind of thing you can't wait too long to do and I ..."

"Good heavens." Bettison's eyebrows flew up. He sat back, clasped his hands across his chest, and gazed at her. At last he shook his head. "Should you? After your surgery?"

"*Because* of the surgery maybe. I'm confident I can do it now, and it might be better sooner than later. But I'd need a few weeks, to prepare and do it, and then make sure *Trink*'s safe 'til I pick her up again. Three, three and a half weeks, perhaps?" With weekends added it would be a month.

"Ahh, I see." He nodded at the pile of files on his desk and coughed. "Pick her up again. So you're really asking for *two* several-week periods off. Well, your circumstances are a little bit special ... perhaps we can push things around a bit. Won't help your career, you know. But granted, unless I change my mind." He chuckled at his joke. "And I will want to know at the earliest when and how long and ... I'll need time to arrange things, and so will you. I am sure the preparation is very lengthy."

Aria stood up and leaned over his desk to shake his hand. "It will be but can be done on weekends—all but the last of it. Thank you, Mr Bettison. Thank you so much. It's a dream for me and this might be my only ..."

"Foolish talk."

"I won't mess you around, I promise ..." she paused, knowing he'd recognise his own joke, "... any more than I have to."

He gave an explosive "Ha!" but his eyes were smiling. "Now—get on with that conundrum. Good morning. Miss Stihl."

Isiah moved to let her pass and she grinned at him. "Did you hear that, Isiah? Vanuatu, here I come."

"You better come to Espiritu. That's my place. Vila's a big bad town, not for you."

"Is it, now? I might like it. Anything's possible."

She was already planning details as she almost danced down the corridor to her office. She was tempted to open a map of the Pacific on her computer and start dreaming about her voyage.

Instead, Aria read the brief.

At mid-morning, she went out to the park below, sat on a bench in the sun and called her sister. "Hey Bree, my plan is coming together. Easter next year, maybe a bit later, I'm going to do that passage to the Islands on *Trinkitat*. Mr Bettison just agreed the time off, this morning. I'm amazed. I expected his reflex 'no' and didn't get it." Her voice was full of laughter and excitement.

There was silence for a while and Aria's effervescence began to fade even before Bree said carefully, "Oh Arz! Don't tell people yet so you can change your mind—you probably will when you've thought about it longer. I certainly hope you will. I think you're nuts."

***

She did, eventually, change her mind but not as Bree hoped. Towards the end of the week, George Bettison called her in again. "Aria, a big client of ours, a property and finance fellow, is rattling his cot sides because he feels we dilly-dally with his work. In general, Gerald deals with him, but Gerald is in court all this week and probably next week as well. It would benefit the practice for you to go over and reassure him ... yes, tiresome, I know. Halaby's his name ... er ..." he peered through the reading lens of his glasses at a scribbled note. "Oh, here. Thadeus Pierre Halaby. He thinks he's such a big shot he needn't bother coming here; Gerald goes to him. But you can afford to take a breather. Go and see the wretched fellow, will you, and convince him that he gets a good service with us? Hmmm?"

David Tobemory was standing at the door, as she went out, giving it a soundless knock. "Lucky old you, Aria. Haha." David had a way of talking soundlessly too.

Aria scowled. "Not in my job description, Tobes; I'm being used." She thought Bettison probably picked her because he considered a charm offensive would work best on this client, but had not dared spell that out to her.

Bettison was close to retirement and not so much sexist as carelessly old-fashioned. He ignored new ideas unless they were to do with law, then showed himself to be right up with modern thought.

She resolved to wait a couple of days on principle, but Bettison doggedly followed up after only a few hours and she agreed to go next day to the offices of Inna Investments. She checked to see that Gerald's actions had been timely.

****

Next day was clear and warm and she looked out at the harbour with longing. Surely, she thought as she dressed, Bettison knows I will deal with this head on; there will be no charm, just reason and facts. She put on a severe dark grey suit and white

Chinese collared blouse that she usually wore to court. She drew her hair up into a French roll and pinned it tightly.

Halaby's office surprised her; it was in a low old building in a small lane off Hobson Street. When his secretary slid his halting door open, saying, "Bettison Weaver Jones' representative, Miss Aria Stihl, sir," and ushered her into his office, Aria got a shock. It was the objectionable idiot from the yacht club. Aria hesitated—just a beat—then strode purposefully across to him.

He rose, stretching out his hand to reveal gold cufflinks set with amethysts. They matched his dark purple silk cravat. "Well, what a delightful surprise! I am pleased to see you again." Aria did not shake hands. He smiled broadly and stepped out from behind his desk to reveal dark purple brogues. "Now, you wished to see me?

A flashy dresser; that fits, she thought. "Good morning, Mr Halaby".

"Call me Thad. They pronounce it Ted here; I guess you'll call me Ted, too. Fine. And your name is Aria? That's a delightful name." In his mouth, it was not—it came out as Orya.

Aria ignored his effusiveness and sat uninvited. He moved back behind his desk. She wished she had worn a suit with a slightly longer skirt and wished even more she had refused to do Bettison's soothing-by-female-hand. "My principal, Mr Bettison, tells me you are dissatisfied with our service—that you find us slow." She paused. Just as he was about to speak, she cut him off to continue, "I have come to assure you that if we take extra time over preparation of material or briefs, it is to be absolutely sure we have covered all aspects and presented all matters ..." She was laughing inside, but kept a straight face.

"Orya. Orya, stop. Life is a joke; we are not meant to take it seriously. Bettison Weaver Jones is a joke too, and the other joke is that I'll complain from time to time to keep them awake but I'll prob'ly keep using them. They know too much already, haha! I suggest you tell Bettison or Weaver or whoever that this was a difficult but successful assignment, and we just go and drink coffee and talk yachts. What do you say? Whatever you say, I won't listen to any more of that stuff from you. And I *do* want to talk boats."

She sat straighter. Well, there goes my wind; he doesn't really care, she thought. She did not want to chat and be social or owe him a cup of coffee, even a company one.

He came round his desk, gesturing to her to get up, and turned to the door. "Let me take you to a most delightful coffee shop just down Hobson Street. I know you are quite a sailor and I'd be real glad if you'd hear me out on the subject of my yacht".

Was that sarcasm? Aria shrugged and followed him out; she had another hour before she needed to be back in her office. She strode along beside him, keeping slightly ahead, and thinking that after this, with luck, she would never have anything to do with him again. Lucky Gerald's problem.

The coffee shop was on a partial rooftop with a broad view out over the Waitemata Harbour. He was right; it was delightful. She stood gazing out at a sprinkling of small craft, the Devonport ferry, a ship manoeuvring with the aid of tugs and in the far distance, the Waiheke ferry tearing along with a wide straight wake. At last, she made the effort to be pleasant. "If I worked here, I'd be all day watching the water."

"Miss Orya as waitress; hard to imagine." He watched her face. It did not move. "But yep, that's why I come here. The harbour is my inspiration. I worked many years in Qatar, in finance, and there I had a fine view of the harbour—well, the ships and sea. 'Inna' means 'indeed' in Arabic. They use it … well, quite broadly, in the Middle East. For me it underlines the spectacular fun of being alive. Indeed! The big joke of life …" A few words were lost as the waitress arrived and clattered things onto the formica table.

Aria said nothing. He sounded slightly crazy or maybe just egotistic. She wondered if his investment company was above board. He reminded her of some of the white-collar criminals she'd dealt with, those who'd had little idea of how other people think, and no idea at all of how they might feel. They had such inflated egos they were effectively lost to communication.

In the coffee shop, they sat close together over the tiny table. Perhaps he had chosen the place for this reason, too. He asked for his usual—cappuccino and red lamington which he tapped with his fork. He grinned at her. "Don't you just love these Lemonton cakes? Chocolate, raspberry—never yet had one that was lemon."

Aria declined cake and sipped her little cup of cooling black coffee, sitting tall in her chair. The din of voices caused him to lean closer to talk. "I'm curious about your sailing skills— wondering how long you've been sailing?" He was looking up at her, unblinking.

"All my life—well, not *all*." She hugged her memories close and gave a brief version. "On holidays, as a kid. My father had a thirty-six footer and we sailed most weekends. I helped Dad bring her back from Noumea several times—three times. Then once I got my own boat, as often as I can. Just coastal stuff, at present."

"Did you ever do your certificates? Coastal navigation? Ocean-going qualifications? I heard …"

"You were going to tell me about your boat." She did not want to tell him anything about herself.

"I've got two. You're familiar with one of them—my catamaran, *Hubbi's Darling*. HD, I call her. The other, my new baby, is for charter—well, that's my plan—a 46 ft, six-berth Li Lei. I had her built in Thailand. She's …"

Aria's phone gonged out a good imitation of Big Ben. She ignored Halaby and pulled it out of her handbag. "Aria." She listened. "Yes …" She pressed it hard to her ear so Halaby would not hear her caller. "Of course. I'll be right back. Thank you." It was Tobes asking something trivial but anything would do. She swallowed the rest of her coffee and wiggled out from her jammed chair, knees bent. "I must go back to the office. Thank you for the coffee and your time. I'll tell Mr Bettison you are generally satisfied with the service our firm offers. Good bye."

He jumped up, frowning. "I really wanted to talk some more about yachts, and I'm not at all sure you'll give me another chance. Call me, huh?" He thrust his card into her reluctant hand again. "Use the mobile number. Or we could meet at the yacht club. Please."

Please! It sounded strange from him, she thought. She clacked her way out across the polished floor, knowing he was still standing, watching her. One moment he was saying all of life's a joke, the next he was serious, over-keen to talk to her, and begging. She put his card on top of a recycling bin opposite the building door. She did not care if he saw it.

Chapter Four

Instead of pressing **2** for his office, Oscar took the lift right up to the top floor. At the end of the corridor, there was a broad view of the harbour. He was early for work, and stood, legs planted wide, to gaze out over it. The ferries were scuttling around, vaguely obscured by a light misty rain. Ragged fracto cumulus swept past Rangitoto and, up towards the bridge, a great sheet of bright sunlight had torn through the higher cloud, a golden strobe with double rainbow. It looked like the Second Coming in his childhood books and a broad grin spread across his face. He felt a surge of joy in his chest. His father would say it was God pointing out the miracle of the natural world. His grin became a rumbling laugh. God or not, it was good. Boats and sailing, he thought, the obvious thing for me. Why have I been thrashing around with overseas jobs, shifting sideways into auditing and other computer stuff, higher degrees, listening to the uncles tell him to marry and stay in Auckland where the money is? He hadn't the heart to tell his family, who wanted so much for him, that he was bored to death. They were so proud of their wild-boy-made-good that it had never occurred to them that he was losing his soul on the second floor.

***

Aria's fridge door was covered in lists. 'Boat gear', 'Nav. gear', 'Papers', 'Safety stuff', 'Electronics etc.', 'Misc.', and 'To be overhauled'. They were already a mess, with things crossed out, added, and written over.

Bree raised her eyebrows when she saw them. She never called before she came to Aria's flat because Aria liked it when people just dropped in; that was like being on a yacht. Here, they rang a bell instead of coming alongside calling out the yacht name but the same welcome was ready for them. Now Bree read the headings aloud. "You haven't got provisions up here. And you'd better make a list of the lists in case one falls under the fridge." She was still holding a multitude of bags, her fingers white with their pressure.

"Really, I've got it all in my head. *Trink*'s pretty simple, after all. But I can't make a mistake when I'm going to be on my own out there." She resumed preparing a salad on the island bench, her back to Bree. "Are you staying for dinner? You can, can't you? I'll tell you my plans. Then I'll drive you home—you can't manage all that stuff on a bus."

"I'll be fine. But Arz, are you really going to do it?"

"Well, Bettison's agreed to let me take leave. All I need to do is … get ready."

"Arz, what are you proving? That you are a better sailor than Dad? That you are a super-woman? Or do you think you aren't going to live much longer? Is that what this is? The cancer? You think you're not going to last even as long as Mum?" Bree's voice was rising. She had only been in Aria's flat a few minutes and she was close to shouting. She put her bags down on the floor, held a hand to her head for a moment then swept her hair behind one ear. When she let her arm fall, she seemed to crumple down with it. "Arz," she said quietly, "I'm really scared. Why do you have to do it?"

Aria stopped breaking leaves, grabbed her pencil and wrote 'snorkeling gear' on the 'misc.' list. She took another page from her notepad, wrote 'Provs.' and stuck it up, with the pencil in her teeth. "I've just got to, Bree." Through the pencil, it came out as "Ahnnn juh goh hoo, Hree". She took the pencil out. "A single-handed passage is my dream. It's not that dangerous—it's endurance more than anything. That's what I want to know I can do—hang in on my own." Bree did not answer. She's fragile as hell, Aria thought.

Aria sighed. Bree was super-bright and super-dumb sometimes. She went to university at sixteen, did a science degree majoring in chemistry and dropped out of her Master's degree when she'd done a few months. Then, on Manny's suggestion, she joined a training programme with the police in document forensics. She loved it. She told Aria she'd found her niche, but it hadn't made her confident. "You don't have to do stuff alone. I haven't told you, but Mat rings me occasionally and asks how you are and if I think you'd see him. Well, bit more than occasionally. He still adores you, Arz. I know what he did was pretty crass, but he's a nice guy and he really does love you."

"What's that got to do with my sailing, or my plans?" She wondered if she should buy a satellite phone; it would be another expense, but good to have if things went wrong.

Bree coloured a bit and squeezed her mouth sideways. "Well, you could be happy together again if you weren't so stubborn. I don't know—you could have a normal life with him and … be happy. He wouldn't ever do it again if …" she trailed off.

She really means if we had children, Aria thought. "I'm never going to have a normal life again, Bree, and I don't want one. Things have changed for me." She knew she was being too tough on Bree but she ploughed on. "Stuff Mat. Yes, I loved him once, but I don't now. Full stop." She went on with the salad. "You go in for this new age whimsy—forgiveness and redemption and stuff. Not me. I just move on. And I've moved on." Maybe no sat phone, she thought; being out of contact is one of the great pleasures of sailing. She wondered if she would be allowed to clear customs and leave without anything. Not likely.

Her sister's eyes filled with tears, but her voice was belligerent. "Arz, you don't care about anybody, but you're all I've got. You aren't *fair* to do this."

Aria stopped breaking pale witlof leaves and turned to look at her. "Bree. For God's sake, it doesn't mean I don't care about you. You know I do." She put her arms round her, patting Bree's shaking back. "But we each have a life, and we do different things. Nothing will happen. I'll just sail up there and fly back. Then the reverse, or I might do some sailing up there, but I'll always be here for you, if you need me. I also have to do my own stuff. And this breast cancer thing is just something I have to deal with. I'll know more after my five year check, and until then, I'll watch out for signs and have fun while there's none."

Bree felt Aria's strong voice vibrating against her chest and longed for it to be her mother's. She could not stop her tears. First her mother, now Aria.

Aria held her a minute longer then pushed back and pulled a wry face. "Hell, you've always got Carlotta—and the magnificent Mr Manny. That should do for a fortnight, three weeks."

Bree did laugh, then, snorting her tears away. "Yep, Carlotta's good. But Manny—I can't factor Manny in. He's with me but he isn't here for me, you know?"

"Then you're wasting time." She paused to let that sink in, then shrugged her shoulders; how many times had she said it?

Bree nodded.

"Oh what the hell, you're twenty-two. You've got time to waste, I guess. Once you're thirty … I just know I want to get out and achieve something. I need to do something difficult and challenging, like single-handed sailing, after this last year, and the Mat thing ….” She pushed the finished salad aside and put an arm round Bree again. “It’s all okay—okay?”

Bree did not answer.

Aria dropped her head against Bree’s hair, and felt a wave of disappointment. “Alright, I’ll agree to put off the single-handed passage. Not next year. But before the five years. Let’s see.”

Bree whispered, “Thanks, Aria.”

Aria touched a pack of two steaks on the kitchen bench. “Damn, let’s sit on the porch for a bit and let them warm; they’ll just poach if I throw them in the pan too cold.” She took out some red wine, bumped the cupboard shut with her knee and hooked two glasses off the rack with her other hand.

Bree reached out but Aria was past her. She trailed after Aria and leant on the rail. “I envy you this view. I should have got a smaller place.”

“Well, this is small, but that’s one thing being on a boat teaches you—it’s not how little you have, it’s how little you need. *Trink* does her best to keeps me poor, of course. I haven’t kept a specific record of what I’ve spent on *Trink* and her berth; I don’t want to know.”

Bree looked at the bottle of wine. “Could be the pinot noir as well. Oh, Arz, I know sailing’s what makes you happy. I miss Dad’s boat. I wish I’d gone out more when I had the chance. Now your damn boat doesn’t have room for anyone else.” Bree threw herself down in a chair and reached for her glass.

“Of course she does. You can come whenever you like. You and I can fit in easily. Just don’t bring Manny. I’m not making space for that waste of …”

“You’ll get your wish, I think. Manny is acting pretty strange. He’s always busy weekends, that hasn’t changed, but now he turns up late, goes away to take phone calls … he’s kind of very absent.”

"Hah. That's not acting strange; that's a new woman. They go like that."

"I don't think it is. But just so you know, I don't think he'll be around much longer."

"Good."

"But I'm scared about that, too."

Aria gave an exaggerated groan and they laughed together as she went in to cook.

Later, they drove through the black streets to Bree's house and Aria watched her wave and close her front door. Yes, she thought, I am Bree's second mother. Even though her sister was an adult, it was not a role she could drop; she must do her best for her. She was right to give in to Bree's wish, she knew, but a heavy cloak of disappointment settled on her shoulders.

On her way home, she glanced at the few people on the streets and thought how desperately lonely a big city could be. At sea, she was very aware of being alone, but never lonely. Somehow the slicked tarmac, the shuttered shops with 'no cash on premises' signs, the kids in hoodies and the grip of their hormones, all made a great bubble of loneliness well up. She did not want to give up her plan; she did not want to spend her life in places like this, only escaping on weekends.

***

Early next morning, Aria stood on her balcony looking down over the rooftops to the harbour. It was a still day; already a few little boats were sailing languidly close in, and the usual armada of fizzies were careering about. The balcony went round two sides of her flat, and had high wind breaks at the ends, so it often had a spot for her chairs that was sheltered whatever the weather. Occasionally something came roaring down from the tropics and struck from the north or northeast. Then the balcony was unusable and Aria watched the drama unfold from inside.

She loved the changes in the weather. She knew she would have been happier being a meteorologist than a lawyer, but somehow, once she'd told her father she was considering law and he'd been so proud, she'd been unable to go back on it.

He'd been a tough but wonderful father. It was fifteen months since he'd died and all that ghastly collapse had been packed into the last eighteen. She shook her wind-tossed hair, dragged her fingers through it and remembered to feel gratitude. She started listing, touching her fingers: grateful for having had parents like Tom and Margie, for her loving sister, for being alive and well again, for the view of the harbour, for Carlotta's special friendship, for her education and a boss like Bettison, for friends and *Trink* and a decent mooring, for meeting Oscar … "Ha, that's stretching it!" she said aloud. She gave the harbour one last scan and went in smiling.

Chapter Five

Aria chugged back into her berth at noon on Sunday and had a good clean up below. In lockers that she had never fully cleared out, she found an assortment of flags, tools, manuals and spares. It was too much to sort on the small saloon table on *Trinkitat* so she bundled it into bags and brought it home. As she piled it into her car, a strong jolt shook the ground. She ignored it.

The boat gear made an awful mess on the living room floor but Aria loved the shippy smell of the old flags and manuals, and needed to catalogue the tools and spares. Her phone began buzzing in the kitchen.

"Hi Tobes. I do hope you're going to say that little seismic jolt dropped the office."

"Haha. Hey, I'm sorry to call you at home," David Tobermory rasped softly. "That Halaby called the office late Friday and wanted to speak to you. I forgot about it."

"I'm sure he can wait. Thanks."

Tobes' soundless laugh somehow made its way down the line. "Is that thanks for the delay?"

"Perhaps. I'll just wait for him to call again."

"Sure. Only thought I should let you know. Hey, we've got a few people coming over. Do you want to join us for a barbie?"

Aria looked at the mess around her. "Thanks, Tobes, but I've just turned my flat into a tip, with stuff off my boat …" She was thinking that sorting old yacht junk might be more fun than the jolly couples at Tobes' barbeque, the men too watchful of anyone single, the women too watchful of their men.

"See you tomorrow then, Aria, office still standing."
David's papery laugh was only just audible.

***

Kyla, the Australian receptionist, dashed into Aria's office on perilous heels. "Aria? There's a call from Mr Halaby? Gerald's client?" She grinned. "The one you went to see?"

"Yes, Kyla. Thanks."

She waited for the phone to flash. Kyla could not walk very fast in such high heels. She pictured Halaby in his office. "Some fellows," Aria could hear her aunt saying in her prim way, "Need a firm hand." This is one of them, she thought.

"Aria Stihl speaking."

"Orya! Hey, great to get hold of you. You're one elusive lady. I called last week and missed you. I've a proposal I'd like you to consider. It's sailing but I really need to explain it to you. I kinda think you'll love it—it's your thing. Can I catch up with you on the weekend? You gonna be around? It's a fantastic idea. You wait!"

He didn't sound like a stalker; more like an excited schoolboy. And she was curious. "I'll be back in the marina Sunday afternoon—probably not 'til about three. I could meet you in the club rooms after four maybe."

"Sure. I'll be there."

***

When Aria brought *Trinkitat* round onto her marina finger late on Sunday, she saw Ted Halaby and Oscar sitting on *Pssst!*'s cabin top. As she cut the motor and nosed gently into her berth,

Oscar gave a feline leap off *Pssst!* and sprinted down the pontoon to catch her lines. He wrapped them onto the bollards and grinned across at her. "Hi! Just showing the boss how slick I am with a line."

"Boss?"

"That's Ted, the guy who owns *Pssst!*. Not exactly m'boss, but I'm getting more and more work out of him. Pays well." He took her spring lines and obeyed her gestures indicating where she wanted them and how loose.

Aria's stomach sank. "I'm supposed to meet him this afternoon to discuss something to do with his boat or … something." So it was Ted Halaby who owned *Pssst!*. He was all but her neighbour in the marina. Damn. She'd only seen Oscar there. "I'm going to tidy up below. I'll come over when I finish, tell him. At least I can avoid having a drink with him if I don't meet him in the club."

"You know him? How come?"

Aria did not answer straight away. "I'll tell you."

"Hang on." Oscar went back to Ted for a moment, then jumped aboard *Trinkitat* and settled himself on the sofa. He filled a fair bit of space in the tiny cabin. "So tell me how come you know this guy. But first, tell me your name. I don't even know that yet."

"Oh, of course." She felt her cheeks flush. "I'm Aria Stihl. I'm a lawyer at Bettison Weaver Jones, a barrister. I live in St Mary's Bay. Umm … that's about it. You can see my place from here." She waved her hand vaguely.

"I didn't know what to call you. I suppose you're the Orya Ted's been talking about today. Am I deciphering his accent right?"

"Yes. But it's Aria. Starts with A." Aria looked at him. He had what people called a chiselled face, each feature well defined in a classic Polynesian mould. His eyes were big and well-spaced, his nose long, his lips full and very clearly delineated. He looked like an intricately carved tourist mask. She broke into a smile and his face, too, lit up. She pumped water into the kettle and lit the primer. "I drink tea when I first get in. You want some?" She tipped leaves into the palm of her hand. "Well, Ted, whose name is actually Tad. I met him in the yacht club after he had nearly collided with me in the channel. He seemed to have no idea of what he'd done. No idea that our boats were both in danger, no idea that someone might have been injured or drowned. Just treated it as a joke. That was just a couple of weeks back, when I was coming in from Opua."

"Hah! Really? I thought he just had brusque manners." He accepted the tea and she pottered about while drinking hers.

"It's more than a lack of manners. He's an *idiot*." She was rewarded by his laugh which changed his face from interesting to marvellous. "I then had to see him for work. He's a client of BWJ's. It didn't wipe out my first impression."

He nodded. "Well, there's always some of those—perhaps sailors are no different. Sort of hoped I'd get on with him somehow." He drank his tea quickly and got up. "I'd better get back. Come over when you feel ready to deal with him. And thanks."

She took her time. *Trinkitat* was pretty tidy—nothing wet, nothing thrown to the floor, no water in the bilge. Below, it was just a matter of packing up leftover food, washing the mugs, plugging the sink, closing the seacocks and forward hatch. She stuffed her personal gear into her seabag and threw it onto the finger. On deck, she coiled lines, put the winch handles away and finally, hosed the cabin top and deck. Oscar and Ted sat watching. She chatted a little while with the two boys on the boat behind her who had seen orcas off the Noises.

When she finally walked over to them, Ted patted the cabin top close beside him. "Come aboard, Miss Orya! You take mighty fine care of your little yacht." She assumed he meant she had taken mighty fine care to keep him waiting. "Oscar here and I were just talking about what to do with *Pssst!*, but let's go below and get a drink and I'll explain."

Aria didn't move. "I don't want anything, thanks. Just had tea. I'm fine."

"Grab a couple of beers, would you, Oscar? We put the beer off when Oscar said that was you acomin' in, but I could do with one. Nothing?"

"No thanks." She sat on the cabin top, more than a metre from him.

"I was saying to Oscar, I'm gonna take *Pssst!* up to Fiji and charter her. Can't be sure I'd get a share of the clientele here. There's plenty of competition there, too, but it's big with resorts and you get a good long sailing season. I been looking into it— way to go, I'd say. Besides, I could do with some sailing in the tropics myself when it's miserable here." He laughed, more of an exclamation than a laugh. "I'm Canadian, though. I know what miserable is."

"And?" She did not look at him, but could feel his eyes on her.

"Well, I thought I'd offer you a job, delivering my beauty …" patting the cabin top, "… to Fiji, if you've got the necessary bits of paper. You never did tell me, but you obviously have the skills. You got Ocean Going whatever? What do you need?"

Aria turned slightly away from him because she could not help smiling at the thought of being offered a job as skipper. "I have my Ocean Going Yacht Master's, unless it's changed in the last few years. So much tech change happening that I should be checking often, but I don't have much stuff on *Trink.* Well, none, so I don't bother." She shrugged. "What you need, I don't know. I think you just call yourself skipper. It would be my first delivery voyage. You realise that?"

"I thought so. But you've done blue water before; that's good enough for me. Question would be, can you get her ready?"

Aria shook her head. "I haven't said I'll take the job. And if you're wise, you'll look for someone who's done one before. But yes, I could probably ready her, with trade help as need be."

"Well? Is it a deal?"

"Of *course* not." She did not mean to sound quite so sharp. "I have a job, various commitments. I can't just drop things and mess about in boats."

His face creased up with amusement. "Isn't that what you do with most of your time already? Apart from when you're working or … attending to other commitments …" He put a slight question in it.

He was fishing. She took care not to bite. "If I do the delivery, it won't be before Easter next year. If you find someone else before then, fine. I'll think about what it would entail and if I decide to go ahead, I'll let you know soon." Aria was already thinking, why not? A paid holiday and a good dummy run for my singlehanded passage. Of course, it would depend on Bree accepting it.

He stood and extended his hand to shake hers. She pretended it was an offer to help her up and jumped to her feet. She turned away to gaze up at the rigging. "I'd like a good look over the whole boat, and I would expect you to slip her, so I see her out of the water. And she's properly maintained."

"Well, Oscar knows more about her than I do. He's been up there." He waved towards the main mast. "And under her. I'll be gittin' along. He'll show you. And it's a good chance to get to know him if he's going to crew for y…"

"Listen!" Aria put her hands on her hips. "If I'm to be captain, I'll make decisions like that, not you. Let's first see if I'm doing it, then *I'll* tell *you* who my crew will be."

Ted gazed at her, laughing openly. "Well hell. I guess you will! Au revoir, Captain." He touched an imaginary cap and stepped onto the finger, still laughing.

Aria waited until Ted was out of earshot and stuck her head over the companionway. "Forget the beer, Oscar. I've seen him off." She watched until he was out of sight, then swung down the companionway. "So! That's who owns *Pssst!*. Small world, eh?" She looked around. "Oh, he's had her done out nicely. The Asians really go to town with the interior woodwork. That would cost a gadzillion here. Elegant and shippy. I like it!"

Below, *Pssst!* seemed huge. At the bottom of the companionway, a big galley lay to port, with a prettily arched entrance to a low cabin under the cockpit. To starboard, a bosun's locker took up half the space the galley did, and the navigation table was set athwartships to take up the other half. In front of that, the saloon was upholstered in dark green velvet with bright-flowered cushions. Aria picked one up and ran her hand over the embroidery. "Flowers are bad luck on a boat … or maybe that's only real ones." The starboard settee was longer than the port one. She went forward to peer into the cabin to port. "Luxurious! But then this squeezy little head and shower. That marks her down a bit, for charter." She stuck her head into the forward cabin. "She's beamy. I wonder if she's good in a sea."

"We might both find out. He's trying to talk me into crewing when he finds someone to do it. I'm not sure I'd be game if it's going to be you."

"I'm like that with idiots. That guy's an idiot. And I didn't mean you can't crew, Oscar. I just wanted to get him straight on who'll make the decisions." Oscar must have heard her conversation with Ted during his protracted look for beer. She let her eyes wander around again. "Ted's got a way to go with her. This boat is practically bare and he's talking about sailing her to Fiji."

"He's aware of that. He was talking about fitting her out for it. You're going to do it, I gathered."

"Haha. Well, someone will, but if I sail her, I would want to know everything about her. I'd started planning a singlehanded passage up there, or to Tonga or Vila, in *Trink*. I have all but got leave arranged for it, in April next year. Maybe a bit later. But my sister's really upset and panicky about it, so I've said I won't do it. Maybe if I did this first ..." She sighed and leaned against the pillar. "It's possible. If I square it with her and I do it, what would you say to crewing?"

His eyebrows lifted. "Well, that's easy. I'll crew for you." He turned to the refrigerator, but Aria caught his broad grin. "Would you like that beer?"

"Come out on *Trink* one weekend. Show me your paces and get some sailing practice. Trink's a bit weird of course, being rigged for single-handing but weird's fine, and it's good training. I'm just going to have a look through aft."

She found another head with a shower over it to starboard, under the cockpit coaming. It was walk-through, the step down and up a minor trap, and led to some storage and hanging space for the captain's cabin, and beyond that, the spacious captain's quarters. An athwartships bunk took up the space against the bulkhead of an aft lazarette. To port, there was a very narrow folding door through to the quarter berth aft of the galley, that would allow quick access to the engine from either side. This might be a hot berth with the engine going, Aria thought, but a better berth in a sea.

She went through. Sliding panels revealed the engine compartment; no space had been wasted. Arriving in the galley, she shook her head. "Bit odd, the captain's cabin having the bunk athwart. I guess you just issue the skipper a warning every time you tack to avoid a head injury. Lovely woodwork, isn't it? The arches are a cute touch."

Oscar watched her while he took a long draught of beer. "You like her. You're picturing yourself sailing her. I reckon you're gonna do it, eh?"

Chapter Six

At work all week, Aria struggled to keep her mind on her cases. On Friday evening, she put aboard *Trinkitat* enough food for two in a chilly-bin and left a note for Oscar on *Pssst!*. She did not know his mobile number, where he worked, or even his surname. It read, "If *Trink* and dinghy are here, come over. A." She sealed it with sticky tape so that Ted, if he came down to his boat, would not read it. Then she went back to her little retreat, snuggled into her smelly old sleeping bag and listened to the ticking on the hull, the occasional tink of a miscreant halyard and a peal of distant laughter as she fell asleep. There was nowhere in the world she felt more content.

Before daylight broke on Saturday morning, she put her tender over the side of the pontoon and rowed up harbour to a scatter of yachts on buoys. The tide was ebbing and against her at first, and it was a hard haul to reach the bridge. It eased off for the turn, as she slipped into the shady stretch with its roar of traffic, and the dinghy slid more easily through the water.

By the time she reached her friend Carlotta's boat, the stream was ripping in and she almost overshot. Aiming to collide, she shipped her oars, grabbed the gunwale standing and shouted, "Aboard *Chicago Gal*!" She gripped tight and pushed out, preventing her dinghy from striking Carlotta's hull.

Carlotta leaped up the companionway, greying curls a mess and plump face split by a delighted grin. "Come aboard! Fanny,

Aria, you coulda brought *Trink* up. There's plenty of water, you know. You don't have to bust ya stitches to get here!" 'Fanny' was Carlotta's way of swearing. She was raised in a convent in Chicago and the girls had been punished for it. Carlotta loved the word, even though she knew most Kiwis considered it obscene.

Aria laughed as Carlotta dropped her fenders. "Hi, Carlotta. Yes, I know, but rowing's good for me. I'm toughening up. Hey, how was your Whitianga trip?" She swung up onto *Chicago Gal's* deck. If she did not fully straighten her left arm, she could take her own weight on it. It felt good after the hard exercise, and she stretched both arms back behind her, hands clasped.

Chicago Gal gave a few exaggerated bobs as a motor boat roared by with a broad wake.

"Ah, y'know, I just gotta get out there every once in a while. It's one thing sittin' here on the *Gal*, and quite another to feel the swell under her. Went up round the Flaxes on the way out. Took the long way round, haha! Didn't put down anywhere cos I got no detailed charts for anywhere much. Circumnavigated the Barrier on the way back and stayed a bit in Fitzroy. Pretty spectacular, the ole Barrier. I didn't spend too long with Harky; just enough time to catch up. Lovely guy," she shrugged, "Pretty lonely but he says that's how he likes it. Suits me."

Aria smiled. Carlotta was not as cynical as she tried to sound. Aria thought she probably really cared about Harky, but just couldn't live with him or live ashore or leave *Chicago Gal*. "Whatever."

"You want a cup of coffee?" Carlotta waved an arm at the hatchway and started down. "Harky's still trying to talk me into a trip up to the tropics again. Can you imagine? Us two old things, in this old boat?"

Aria could hardly hear her. She followed her down the companionway. She had seen Harky many times, and Dad had known him well. He always struck her as an unlikely subsistence farmer because he had such a gentlemanly air of orderliness, of organisation.

"Why not? If you went over her 'til she was in tip-top order, picked your time and took it easy, why couldn't you do it? But wait 'til …"

"Nah! All very well to dream, but I'm not sure I'd ever get the *Gal* into shape. Or myself, to sail that far!" Carlotta was a middle-aged nurse, originally from Chicago. She had sailed to New Zealand and worked to buy an old but neat little single-hander, re-naming her *Chicago Gal*. She was the only other female single-hander Aria knew.

Aria dropped onto a settee and watched Carlotta grinding coffee in a machine from a previous age.

She had crewed for Aria's father, Tom, on many races, and nursed him in his final weeks at the old Stihl home. Carlotta had caught the tail end of the hippie era, free love and all that. He was quite a bit older than Carlotta and appreciated her energy and kindness. After her mother died, Tom had been desperately lonely but equally desperate to do the right thing by his daughters.

Aria waited 'til the racket of the grinder stopped. "I knew Harky sailed out from England and to the Islands but not much more. I think England is hard to go back to after experiencing the tropics."

"Experiencing the tropics or the women of the tropics? Haha. Whatever; they don't go back. You know, I figure the Poms colonised the world because they couldn't face that climate again! I was there a year, at a hospital in Birmingham. Not as cold as Chicago, but a lot drearier. And they're not too impressed by Americans."

Aria laughed. "Well, if you need some sunshine, consider this: I'm thinking of doing a trip to Fiji—a delivery job."

Carlotta's hands stopped. She opened her eyes wide and mouthed, "Fanny!" Then she yelled, "You're gonna do whaaaat?"

"I had that week off and sailed up to Opua easily enough. Stiff blow coming back in, no problem either. I seem to be fine. I need to be even fitter and stronger, of course … but listen, this guy has offered me a job delivering his yacht up to Fiji." She leaned forward. "Lotta, I think I might do it. It's paid, the yacht is a good size and new. She was built in Thailand and brought out here on a ship. I suppose she'd have had sea trials and everything there. I don't know much yet. But it's tempting. I wondered … if I did do it, would you crew for me?"

Carlotta had been staring at Aria with her mouth slightly open. With a yell, she threw a tea towel at the coach roof. "Fanny! Would I what! Whoohoooo yep! It's a few years since I've done any ocean stuff. The *Gal* is past it but I'm not—I'm in!"

"Hang on! I haven't said I'll do it. It depends on a lot of things, not least whether the boat's seaworthy. *Looks* a nice boat. But she's bare and I think hasn't moved, here. I have to be sure she's safe, of course. And I need to get enough time off work, though Bettison has already agreed to some. Bree's acting up big time. Double that if you're away too …"

"Fanny, she's not going to be bothered about me being away. She never comes to see me. She never even rings or …"

"Hah! What use would that be? You have your damn phone switched off. And how would she visit you, for goodness sake? I have to row up here. How does the hospital get hold of you?" Carlotta was a highly skilled nurse but chose irregular hours and on call work because it gave her the flexibility to live on and look after her yacht. She did at least have an outboard motor on her dinghy.

"They hang a sheet out the window."

"What! They signal you? They shouldn't employ you—they must see you're a nutter. Stuck in the past as well. Signalling's completely primitive."

Carlotta was screaming with laughter. "If it works, don't re-invent it. When it's blowin' hard enough to flog the sheet, they know not to bother; I'm gonna be out here lookin' after the *Gal*. I got 'em trained."

Aria gave the slow head-shake of disbelief. "Well, I'm not sure I'll even do it yet, and this owner creep is already telling me who my crew will be, and I am not having that. I'll decide who I sail with, not him. I want to sort that out before I say yes."

"Ok, but I'm in. That's the best offer I've had for a long while. A creep? Then why are you dealing with him?"

"Well maybe that's the wrong word. He's a very annoying guy; he has a presumptuousness, a my-way-or-no-way thing about him that irks me. But I want to do the job, in spite of that. I want to show Bree I can do it before I go single-handing. She's in such a tizz."

"So, two reasons. You want to do it, and you got him under your skin but need to show him first off that it will be *your* way or no way. You're prob'ly two peas of a pod."

"Not likely. I don't fancy him at all. Bree does, thinks he's good looking."

"So the deal's all but done. Well, I'll have to come down to see the thing before it's really done. No use getting' out there and finding you don't like the boat or you don't think she's safe." Carlotta peered out a porthole. "You want to hang around until nearly the turn, or row home against it and get a lotta tough'ning up? I got a few jobs you could help me with. There's a slight leak from the stern gland—nothin' much, but nothin' at all would be better."

"I certainly will. Deferred maintenance is *non*-maintenance, Lotta."

Together, they repacked the stern gland as best they could and bailed out the bilge. Then they put a new washer in the bilge pump, and replaced the gungy-brown filter in the freshwater one.

Carlotta poured boiling water into the cold coffee.

Aria sighed and threw herself down on the settee again. "How long's all this stuff been waiting? Who knows what's in your tank. I might not have drunk your coffee if I'd seen that filter first. You should slip her, Lotta, clean her up properly and sort the stern gland out better. Easier than bucketing and waiting to find your feet get wet."

"I pump the bilge every week. I've been using the hand pump, so it's good we fixed the proper one. Yeah, I know, she needs slippin'. It's all dough though, and once she's up, you gotta keep shellin' it out until she's all done, in the shortest possible time. Difficult. I'm savin' up. But if I go with you, I'll put her up on the hard. Have the stuff done, and save havin' to find someone to look after her."

"I'll help you with the cost if need be but I'll tell Ted he's got to pay the crew. See what happens; I've an idea he likes to play the big man."

"Fanny! That'd be great. I'd have come anyway, but *paid* … oh, yes Ma'am! I'll be in for that. Can't wait!" She peered out to check the movement of the tide.

Aria set off when the out-running tide picked up, and rowed easily down to the marina. She threaded her way between manoeuvring yachts. On her pontoon, she saw Oscar watching her. He was bare chested and his long dark hair was gleaming on his shoulders. In the bright sunlight, his teeth were startlingly white, and his eyes, too, when he raised his eyebrows in greeting. Just an inch of tattooing showed above his board shorts.

She paused. He's magnificent, she thought.

Chapter Seven

Oscar was standing tall, eyes wide in greeting. "Aria! I got your note, eh."

Aria waved, tied the painter and climbed aboard *Trinkitat* before she turned to him. "Hi. I didn't know how else to contact you. You're still Mystery Man. And I wanted to ask if you'd like to come out sailing.

"You're going out today?" He was shifting from one foot to the other.

"Yep. Round Little Barrier and to Fitzroy. Well, no, it's actually too late for that now."

"It's mid-day. You going to overnight? I've got the basic stuff with me—asked Ted if I can sleep aboard. I like that ticking noise and the slight rocking, eh. I didn't know about that. I've been out on a lotta boats at home but never slept on one. I've got a sleeping bag and some sandwiches—they're, umm, all cheese." He shrugged. "I can eat cheese sarnies for two days no prob. Pretty easy kai." He gave a deep rumbling chuckle that made her smile. He was like a boy with a man's full size laugh.

"I put enough food aboard in case. Oh, unless you're supposed to be working on Ted's boat." Aria started backing down the little companionway.

"No, he didn't ask me to do anything. I suppose I should be alarmed; allowed to sleep on board when there's no work. The old concept of indebtedness."

Aria did not understand what that meant. "Well, I'd say watch him."

Oscar grunted. "I'll get my stuff. We going now?"

Aria looked at *Trinkitat*'s clock and grimaced. "Lunch on the way to wherever. It's a southerly, so nowhere's going to be really good. We'd make Tryphena before dark. The forecast's alright for today, but tomorrow, a front's coming through, late morning."

"Is that a plan or a few vaguely connected ideas?" His eyebrows were up, forehead wrinkled, eyes laughing.

"We'll do Shoal Bay, the south east corner of Tryphena Harbour, because it's closest. It rolls in there too but should be manageable. Sound like a plan now? Let's get going." She put her mug on the dishcloth in the sink. "The dinghy goes upside down under the boom. Then we'll throw off the springs. I just leave them until I get back."

Once they were under way, she continued. "The usual rules apply. Only three knots, bowline, reef knot, round turn and two half hitches. Whatever fancy ones you've learned, forget them. And if I find a granny, you're finished. No leaning over the rails, no sitting on the safety lines, use the head and remember that women and sailors sit down. The rest I'll tell you as we go."

Oscar nodded and grinned.

Aria steered the whole way, only getting Oscar to help with the sails and make tea. She kept up a commentary on what she was doing and why. He appeared to be listening; perhaps he didn't dare not.

"The Colville Channel will be rough today. Better eat something now, before it's too bad."

Oscar made tea and brought out cheese sandwiches. Uhuh, Aria thought, treble the rations for a Fiji trip if he comes. Carlotta would stay plump while eating like a bird, but this guy would demolish the stores and stay skinny.

As they crossed the Colville Channel, occasional large waves slapped and rolled them, crossing the wind-driven ones from the south. Dolphins sprang up from astern and sped past them, jumping in their bow wave and crossing ahead at wild speed. Oscar picked his way carefully forward and heard Aria calling to them, "Te puhi!" Spray flew high over the coach roof and Aria shouted, "Remember one hand for the boat!"

When he came back, he murmured, "*Listen, for like a golden snake / The Ocean twists and stirs…*"

"Oh, that's Flecker, isn't it? They still do that in school?"

"I'm a while out of school. But yeah, we were expected to read the English classics—mostly the morbids. *O for the touch of a vanished hand* … part of having a stuffy-school education." He grinned and shrugged. "I loved it; it has a music to it and I can still get high on my favourites. But there's some fantastic moderns too; the magpie poem and all that."

Aria looked at his classic Polynesian face in profile. Who would have thought he'd be into poetry?

Rounding into Shoal Bay, Aria started her motor and continued with her instructions, yelling into the wind. They dropped the main and went close in to allow for drifting back once the head sail was furled. Aria ran up to the bow and dropped the anchor herself. "Good chance of losing a finger first time you do that."

Oscar had tossed many an anchor over, but did not tell her.

The southerly had swept them across in one broad reach with the wind on the starboard quarter. Now it sent a small swell rolling round into Shoal Bay. As well, *Trinkitat* was hit by bullets of wind off the high hills, causing her to lurch on her anchor chain from time to time.

Oscar watched as *Trinkitat* danced around on her anchor. "Hey, surely Port Fitzroy would have been better? Not that I ever get queasy."

"No, not really. Fitzroy is more comfortable, but parts of it aren't really good holding at all. We'll be fine." She stretched her stained old cover over the main sail and did up the clips that still worked, dropped and covered the mizzen and looked around, sighing with satisfaction. "Tea, eh? I'm about talked out for the day. You can tell me your name at last." She laughed at the absurdity of not knowing his full name, lifted the tiller to make more room and moved to where she could hear him.

Oscar went below to the galley. "That tiller must be hard work on a day like today." He filled the kettle. "Niu. That's Dad's name, but we were sort of adopted into the 'Sisu family. Complicated, because family's very important in Samoa. I'll tell you the story some time." He made strong tea. "Dad's a pastor with the Samoan church in central Auckland. It's a tough job but he loves it. It's his hobby, really, being Rev. Niu."

"New?" Aria grabbed her phone and woolly hat and went back up.

"N-I-U. You say the vowels almost separately, not quite. Crazy name." He recited his number while Aria tapped it into her phone. "I didn't bring my phone. I like to escape from it."

Aria entered 'Oscar Niu'. She liked the sound of it. "It's a nice name. How did a Samoan come to be called Oscar?"

"Oh, Samoa used to be German once. The story of my family stems from that. Then NZ governed it in various arrangements until they gave it back in '62. The Americans snatched some islands, too, and *haven't* given them back." He pulled a face, then scanned the anchorage as he took the tea back up to the cockpit. "All good?"

Aria nodded. They drank their tea in silence, enjoying the sounds of the anchorage. Aria dropped below. "Thai beef and green papaya salad."

He threw himself back on the cockpit seat. "Whaaat? Too much!" and she blushed. She hoped he didn't think she'd made an extraordinary effort for him. He sat up again. "You always eat fancy stuff when you're sailing? You make this or buy it?"

She put two bowls and spoons on the cockpit floor and carried up tumblers of water.

"Made. Just cook the beef, make the dressing and chuck it all in. I like making treats for little weekend trips. But you won't get anything fancy on an ocean passage. Everyone will take a turn."

"We going? You reckon?" He wished he could pin her down to it. He didn't know how he would get enough leave but he didn't care.

Aria grimaced. "The delivery … well … great opportunity. Suits me if it's paid and it would probably reassure Bree."

"Bree?"

"My sister Aubrey. She's dead against my single-handing. She's much younger than me so things were a lot tougher for her when our mother died, and she kind of clings to me. She's only twenty-two now. But I'll talk to her. My old friend Carlotta says she'll crew if we do it. She's a great sailor, so that'd be a sweet set-up.

"Old? How old?"

"Meaning I've known her since way back, since I was a teenager. She'd be good. Yes, I want to do it but I just have this … background feeling that something's not right or … well, strange."

"Do you?" Oscar looked up, frowning.

"Maybe it's just that Halaby annoys me and he knows it and still asks me to work for him. He's too persistent." Aria frowned, and stared across the darkening anchorage. "Why ask *me* to deliver the yacht? There are plenty of real delivery skippers out there. You just go to Crewbay or one of those websites. There's people who do it professionally through to people who'll do it for nothing. Or he could just get crew and do it himself. He's offered pay, though I don't know how much yet. So it's not that he's looking to economise by getting someone who's not a professional. Is he just trying to get closer to me? Or you? He keeps giving you little jobs to do."

"Not me! Maybe you. Ted's Canadian but … of Middle Eastern origin? And worked in Qatar, he said. He might think that way still. It's different, *incredibly* different. I found it fascinating." Oscar leaned forward. "They have this concept of indebtedness. It preceded money, they say. Money was invented to deal with that so is tied to goods or services. Human interaction, the provision of these, is all about indebtedness. That idea's the basis of sharia banking—and of the hawala system, too, the transference of debt or credit, but they kind of keep a balance sheet of everything in their heads."

"What? Really? That must have been weird for you working there." Aria reached for the salad and put it in the bowls. "Salad with a spoon. Easier aboard."

It was elegantly chopped and Oscar whistled, murmuring thanks. "Yep, weird. It's social as well as financial. It's what you're worth to them. Ted might think that way. Really hard to understand when you first strike it and it doesn't feel comfortable." He laughed and shook his head. "Odd concept for us."

Aria was staring at him. "For real? Life's a giant balance sheet? I'll have to think about that one."

Oscar watched the other boats silhouetted against the headland as a vicious bullet of wind swept down on the bay. *Trinkitat* jogged but held her position, and he looked back at Aria. "Sort of. All negotiations, all deals, are based on it. Oh, and by the idea that knowledge is power. They sometimes won't shake hands on a deal until they've figured out what you've forgotten or don't know. You have to build a careful loophole in—one that won't get away from you!" Oscar's laugh bubbled up. "But I might be completely wrong about Ted."

"You're not a just little jaundiced, are you?"

"No. Just their culture—it's how things work there. I'm just saying that's how Ted might think. We'd see it in him as dodginess."

Aria pulled the corners of her mouth down. "Dodginess. Well, how can I know? He's one of the wealthier financiers in town; he's one of the movers and shakers, even if he keeps a lower profile compared with some of the others. I'm pretty sure his slate would be clean because Bettison only deals with the good, righteous old stickler that he is." She shrugged. "Maybe it *is* just that I don't understand Ted's way of thinking. But I feel a bit … well, not stalked, quite, but pursued."

"Yeah, I think you maybe are. But a delivery voyage—how problematic can that be?" Oscar's deep laugh was barely audible.

"*Very*, sometimes."

"Working for him, I meant. The sailing part, yes. I've been reading stuff about deliveries and they have their own unique problems, I gather."

"Certainly do. I think some owners avoid doing it themselves because they're not competent. Then they don't know what to look for when choosing crew, either. Ted's probably in that category. And some crews take a 'not my boat, not my problem' attitude. Some skippers, too. They let stuff break, take chances they wouldn't take with their own boat or gear. Give up at the least hitch, abandon ship when she hasn't sunk …"

"So we have to actually sink before you crack out the life raft?" His eyes were laughing.

"Yep. Can't stop the deluge, pumps failed and bailing not beating the inflow, waterline reaching the gunwales—going down, haha!"

"Jeez."

"It won't happen. I'll be properly prepared and we'll take no chances."

"Aah, so you *are* going to!" He grinned at her. "I'm doing my tickets as soon as I can. I've enquired at the Polytech for all three. Every time I do some prac, I have to get the skipper to sign it off. Two sixty mile passages, two over-nights. That isn't just sleeping in Tryphena. And a couple of goes at skippering, gotta have."

"I'll help you. But you must've sailed before. Your skills seem ok. Why didn't you say?"

"Yeah, well, I've sailed all manner of home-built things in Samoa. The cuzzies and me, we spent all our time making rafts, and later va'aalo, outrigger canoes, using them to fish. My aunts used to get frantic, but the uncles just saw it as the ordinary risks of growing up. None of us drowned. So yeah, lots of experience with little boats, and some of the big fishing boats. Everyone's got power boats now, pretty much."

"Well, getting your tickets is a good thing to do, especially if you're not committed to your career."

"Really, I do have to stick with a proper job. I dream of doing something different. I think about all sorts of boat jobs, but I'm the main support for my wider family, so I can only do it on and off. I'm the only one who has a profession, and I lend a lot of money to them that they don't know about." He laughed. "I got the aunts onto Kiva, a sort of Grameen bank online, a micro-lending thing, where people can borrow small amounts for income-generating things. I use a pseudonym—several actually—and lend to them. Not much. Kiva recommends no more than twenty-five dollars at a time, but with lots of people putting in twenty-five … it adds up. They have to make a plan and pay it back. It's been great for my aunts. They're all doing better, all learned how to manage their money."

"Multiple pseudonyms! Who's the dodgy one now?"

"There's no harm in it. Some of them got practically wiped out by the 2009 cyclone, and I just gave them money then, but they don't like to accept it as a …"

"Hah, don't like indebtedness …"

"Yeah, well, not within the family. They're proud people; that's why I do the Kiva thing. I'm KiwiKiddo and Upadollar and Troppo and stuff. They don't have to know. And they've always been so kind to me, it's hard to see them struggling, getting older, kids not able to help, couple of 'em pretty useless. You know how big families go, I guess." Oscar sipped his wine and gazed out into the darkness.

Across the water, voices and laughter drifted in snatches through the clink of halyards. The wind was dropping, no longer gusting. "Not really." There was no moonlight, but the lights of the settlement showed the anchor was holding. Later, it would only be the dark shapes of the hills, the scatter of riding lights, and the stars, if any remained visible.

Oscar followed her gaze. "Maybe get some sleep, eh."

"I just hope the wind doesn't come round later on. We need to keep an eye on the bearing of the hills. Don't put any faith in the riding lights; we might all be dragging together." Aria laughed at a mental picture of it. Oscar looked round the anchorage and laughed with her.

Then she was quiet a long time, struck suddenly with envy of Oscar's sprawling, loving family. She had just Bree, her dear old aunt and two cousins in the South Island who were both married with young kids so she hardly ever saw them. And she missed Mat's family. "No, I don't know a lot about big families at all, not really. Mat had a great horde of relations, but I couldn't spend much time with them. My family's nearly non-existent." She shrugged. "But that's just family; I have friends and they make up for it quite a bit. I'm grateful for that." She gathered up the bowls and salad box and jumped below. She stood in the opening, moonlight falling on her face. "Help yourself to anything you want. I'll keep an eye on the stars out the companionway, while they're there, though I'm sure that won't be long. Usually, I sit up there and whittle. That's one of the annoying noises when she's under weigh, my whittling stuff jiggling about. I can never keep it quiet." She laughed. "But known noises are ok. You can have the quarter berth if you fit in. Just put any gear aside. Good night." She rinsed the bowls and left them in the sink.

Oscar's topknot shone in silvery starlight. "Okay. G'night. I'll watch a bit longer." When he came down later, he saw that he had no hope of fitting into the quarter berth. He moved oilies and jerseys off the settee, and curled up there, but it was also small. He looked across at Aria snuggled into her sleeping bag on the opposite settee. Her face was angled to the companionway, blonde hair falling over her forehead and half a smile lost in sleep.

***

During the night, Aria woke to more vigorous rolling. The wind had returned and strengthened, and through the hatch she saw a small ellipse of sky quickly closed by scurrying cloud. She got up, to find Oscar standing in the cockpit. "You have any sleep at all?"

He jumped. "Yeah, enough. But it's coming over a bit squally. Just thought I'd have a look."

"There was a front predicted. It might be a bit faster and stronger than they thought—more than the 20 to 25 knots they said. What time is it?"

"Four fifteen. You were sleeping like a baby."

"Well, I thought I had one eye open, or one ear. I'll get some tea and breakfast and we'll go, eh?" Soon other boats were starting to move in the darkness. Engines puttered, anchor chains rattled and occasionally, a voice drifted across the darkness. Aria jumped below, switched on the radio and tried to get rid of the static. She put the kettle on and raided Oscar's supermarket bag for more cheese sandwiches. That boy certainly doesn't take a chance with hunger, she thought. "We'll need something under our ribs today! Probably won't get a chance to eat again before we get in." She shelled more boiled eggs, pulled out the now-warm ham slices and washed two tomatoes. "Lunch for breakfast," she said as she put the deep plates on the cockpit floor.

Oscar laughed.

"Here's the forecast …" Aria turned one ear towards the crackling radio wedged into a shelf and repeated it loudly to him."… southerly, 20 to 25 knots, gusting 30 … south-westerly late afternoon and easing… 15 to 20. Seas rough, very rough by afternoon … yep, we'll go now." She brought two mugs of hot tea up with her. "No milk."

"I'm learning not to expect it."

Aria jumped back down the companionway and shouted up to Oscar from the lockers. "Dad's old oily is big enough for you. It has a little tear in the back of one sleeve, but you'll probably only get the spray in your face. We'll do it in four tacks, I reckon, the first three hard to windward." She put on a woollen jerkin, knitted cap and oily top. Her bare legs and feet were impervious to cold as long as her body was warm.

Oscar did not have much choice. He put the old oily over his two sweatshirts and pulled one of Aria's woolly hats on. He took off the tracksuit pants he had slept in and threw them down the companionway, leaving board shorts. "Hope Dad hasn't switched the hot water off and there's a good hot bath at home."

"You still live with your *parents*?" Aria took a cheese sandwich, more cheese than sandwich. She laughed at the thought of him living at home.

"Yeah, I never really moved out. When I was at Canterbury, they kept my room waiting even though I always went home— to Samoa, I mean. Then I worked here in Auckland, same. Went to Dubai for two years; supposed to be one but it took two. When I got back—about three months ago, now—it's all waiting for me. Easy to just settle in again. Yeah, there's a lot of jokes about guys who are twenty-five and haven't left home. The Hotel Mama stuff, but I do pay decent board. Straight to the church, I think. What the hell, I say, if the hot water's not turned off."

Aria pulled a wry face. "I miss those times. Mum died sixteen years ago this month. Dad died last year."

"Oof, that's tough."

Aria did not answer. After a while, she gave a brief nod. "We'll go as soon as we've drunk our tea. Sooner the better, I think. The weather report's never dead accurate. The error might be in our favour and might not. That front is moving faster."

Oscar blew on his tea. "Living at home at a late age has its downsides, though, as you can imagine." The rumbly laugh came through the dark again. Aria thought, I bet that's his father's laugh, too.

Aria put the mugs and plates in the sink on the dish cloth with a tea towel between them. Then she looked at her chart, laid a ruler across it, measured a few angles and jotted some notes on a pad. She stood at the companionway. "Oscar, I've got a high cut sail, a yankee jib, in the forepeak. We'll take off the genny and bend that on and not even put up the main. We'll sort the mizzen later. I'll hand the yankee up. No need to flog ourselves 'cos we've got all day." She went forward, opened the hatch to a belt of wind and grunted as she bundled the sail out of the hatch. "You know how to hank it on?" she called up to him. "Make sure you've got it right way up. There's a yellow patch on the hoist." She closed the hatch and tightened it down, ready for water over the foredeck. It took some time to stow the last few things. She bounded up the companionway. "Up jib and anchor, and we'll sail out."

Oscar lashed the anchor as he'd seen it the day before, looked at the yankee high above him and came back to the cockpit grinning. *Trinkitat* was already heeled over and slicing along before Aria had the sheet properly in.

When Aria had laid their course out of the harbour, the wind biting their faces and legs, Oscar hoisted the mizzen. "Right up. The jib pulls hard and it helps balance her. If there's much of a wind shift, we might have to do a bit more work." Aria's heart was soaring as it always did when she had *Trinkitat* sailing in a good strong breeze.

Dawn was breaking and silver streaks burst through the clouds, even though the sun was not yet rising. To the west, the sky was dark with cloud. Aria kept her eyes ahead, but Oscar watched how fast the light arrived. After a long time, he smiled. "Beautiful, eh. The gold's starting now."

Aria nodded. "Best time of the day. I was never one to lie in bed, even as a teenager. You can't, on a farm. Always loads of things waiting to be done."

"Haha! I was hopeless. It was an early morning part-time job that got me through Uni, I reckon. Without it I wouldn't have got to any morning lectures. Working soon knocks that out of you."

Aria was gazing up again. "We can pinch it a bit more to bring us down closer in. If we get too far over to the west, there's a whole bunch of stuff to avoid north of Motutapu. The Noises, a few islands and rocks." The motion was rough and spray was being hurled right back to the cockpit. "Colville Channel's rough ... further into the gulf we get, the easier it'll be." She hauled the sheet in tighter, causing *Trinkitat* to heel hard and come up closer to the wind. Spray shot higher and water streamed down their oilies and bare legs. Oscar planted a foot firmly against the cockpit seat and thought, it's cold and uncomfortable and she's in her element. This is what she likes, being on one ear in this bloody little thing with the wind in her face.

Later she gave him the tiller and a lot of instructions, and when they passed the channel buoy, he was still steering with a wide grin.

Up the harbour, among the press of yachts, she watched as Oscar negotiated his way. The wind had steadily abated and come round to the south west and he handled it easily.

"You think you can take her in? I'll drop the sails soon and you just motor very slowly." She wanted him to get those tickets.

When they had moored, she gave a thumbs-up and got an impassive face and a sideways nod.

Chapter Eight

Aria drew up behind a shiny red motorbike parked in front of Bree's house in Waterview. Bree had bought a 'deceased estate', dingy and tatty, but it was Art Deco style and Bree loved it. It had both a small view of the Te Atatu arm of the harbour and a neat sloping garden with old trees. While Aria sailed, Bree painted, decorated, played tennis or tended her garden.

The red motorbike would be Manny's and Aria felt the prick of irritation. She wondered if Manny knew that Bree owned the house or thought she rented it. She supposed that Bree, innocent that she was, had probably told him. Maybe she had even told him she had an extra income from Dad's shares. Aria wondered if that was the attraction for him, not just her pliability.

One of Manny's strange habits was to be around only Sunday to Thursday. He offered no explanation for this, just reappeared on Sunday and sometimes took her out somewhere, with or without a group of his men friends.

Aria called hello down the back garden and went to the kitchen to tackle the coffee machine.

Bree came rushing up the garden path calling, "Hey, Arz! You've got to see what I found! Scented clematis! I'm going to put it on an archway. The buds are pink and the flowers white with yellow throats … they're gorgeous!" She looked at Aria suspiciously as she set the coffee on a battered tray. "What are you up to, Arz? You haven't come to tell me you're going after all, have you?"

"Not single-handing, no. I gave you my word on that. But there's another idea afoot. Come on, let's have this in the garden. It might help you stay calm." She picked up the tray and carried it to a table under a gnarled Bramston apple tree where Manny was sprawled in a fraying cane chair.

"Oh Aria, no. Whatever it is, no." But Bree was thinking of the clematis plan and did not sound upset. She reached up and touched an apple blossom on its bare branches. "Thanks for the pastries, Arz, but it makes me suspicious! What's this about?"

Aria wanted to talk to Bree alone. She made small talk with Manny and hoped he would leave. But that was not Manny, she knew; he would wait to hear why she'd come.

"Bree, I've had a job offer, a sailing job." She paused, and Bree waited. "Doing a delivery up to Fiji. It's a big boat, fourteen metres, new and well designed …" She hoped that proved true. "… and if I did it, I'd take crew. Carlotta and a young guy you don't know from the marina. He's a strong, do-everything kind of guy and doesn't get seasick so I think he'd be good. But listen," she slowed down and said clearly, "I won't go if you don't want me to."

Bree was staring at her with big eyes. Manny showed no interest.

Aria took a deep breath and started repeating herself. "It's fourteen metres … lots bigger than Dad's, and new, …"

"How long would it take?"

"About ten days, I'd guess—might be less in a boat as big as that. Yes?" She waited. The sun disappeared.

Bree leaned back with closed eyes. Then she sighed and screwed up her mouth. "Oh Arz, you are so goddamned determined. I suppose I should have known you were going to do *something*. But no, that doesn't scare me half as much.

Carlotta's going? She's a good sailor but isn't she too old for it now?"

Aria shrugged. "I don't know. Don't know how old she is. Late forties, fifties?"

"I don't know either. Lots younger than Dad was."

"I rowed up to her boat the other day. I wanted to get some reliable crew sorted out before I asked you about it and made a decision."

Bree nodded and gave a sad-sweet smile. "Thanks."

"Hey, thank *you*, Bree. It'll be a doddle, I think. Getting ready won't be. It hasn't sailed; it was brought here on a ship, just motored to the marina. You must come down and look at her, after I speak to the owner."

"Who owns her and why don't they do it themselves?"

"A guy called Halaby. Bit of a jerk, really, but he's not coming on the trip, so that's OK." Aria noticed that Manny was suddenly alert and listening intently, gazing ahead but sitting very still. He reminded Aria of an accused in court, when a witness gets close to the crucial evidence. He even breathed stealthily. "Well, that's it really, until I let him know. Then it will be action stations getting the damn thing ready. But we have quite a few months."

Manny yawned and said in a drawl, "When are you sailing?" He had a weird coming-and-going accent.

"Late April. May. Depends on the weather, really. No crew positions available."

"Is that to keep me out or keep Ted out?"

Aria dropped her head on one side. "You know him?"

"Oh yeah, everyone knows this man. He's a very visible jerk." He pronounced it 'zherk'.

Aria stood up. "Hey Bree, I have to run. Drop in soon. But I'll keep you filled in anyway." Aria gave her an awkward hug round the shoulders from the side of the chair, and kissed the top of her head. "See you." She nodded at Manny.

In the car, she wondered how well Manny knew Halaby. Perhaps he had seen her from the yacht club verandah going to *Pssst!*. That meant he knew that *Pssst!* was Ted's boat. It would be surprising. Auckland was a big city; even the marina was a big place and only one of several. A work link? Possible. Manny had a job with some software company. She dismissed it and worked her way home through the traffic as misty rain began to fall.

***

When she had not called after nearly two weeks, Ted Halaby rang the office. Kyla rushed to Aria's room. "Excuse me, Aria? There's a call from Mr Halaby? Can you take it? He's the one…" She stopped and squeezed her lips together, knowing her thoughts were readable.

Aria saved her work. "I'll take it. Thank you, Kyla." She watched Kyla leave and waited for her phone to flash. "Aria Stihl."

"Hey, Orrya!" Ted exaggerated his accent and drawl. "Time's gettin' along and all that. I can imagine you're thrashing a case or two and suffering from your social life but I'm looking for an answer, huh? Have you thought enough yet? I'm offering good pay … you not too busy to talk about it?"

"Good morning, Ted. No, not especially busy. I've decided that I'll accept the job subject to my being satisfied that the yacht is seaworthy, properly equipped and her papers in order. I'd also like to discuss pay with you. My crew would want to be paid as well. There will be two, Oscar, and Carlotta Tedesky. She's a good sailor. She sailed here from the States and she's a nurse. Definite asset."

"A Polish gal? Well, I know you said you wouldn't compromise on crew, but I would certainly like to meet Miss Colodda. Could you arrange that? I'll be down at the marina next weekend. Now I know we're neighbours I can be available pretty much any time weekends." His grin was audible.

Aria wondered if her irritation was audible too. "I usually sail on weekends. But yes, I'll see you then. I haven't had time to look at *Pssst!* much yet." She was tempted to leave the marina this weekend as soon as work finished and not come back 'til Sunday evening.

"Great, Orya. We'll discuss the details then, huh? That's unless you'd like to join me for lunch today—there's a great seafood place near ..."

"Thank you, Ted, but I've a full schedule today."

"Oh, no problem; I just thought as you aren't particularly busy ..." There was laughter behind his words again.

Aria kept her voice flat. "I'll meet with you on the weekend. Sunday afternoon. Bye." She dropped the phone, took a deep breath and hissed it out through her teeth. She wondered if Kyla listened at the door. After a moment, she saw the voyage in her mind. A week or ten days, maybe more. It would be impossible to get good weather for that long, so they would take a blow or two and get a calm in between. You always got a calm. But for her, it would not matter; it would be a magic ten days.

***

On Saturday morning, when she saw Oscar on *Pssst!*, Aria took a good look over the yacht. She scrutinised and fiddled with everything, tested the pumps and the head, leaned on every shroud and looked up at the rigging so long that she rubbed her neck. She uncovered the life-raft and looked at the packing date.

Pssst! had been sitting around for nine months. Halaby had been in no hurry.

Oscar moved softly around behind her, watching, then put his head on one side. "Well?" Neither had spoken for almost an hour.

"Seems fine. There's stuff to be checked and stuff to be got. The first blow will tell us more than any looking can. We'll have to take her out. Okay, see ya!" and she jumped onto the dock and jogged up the pontoon to *Trinkitat*. She heard him laugh.

***

"Carlotta. This is Aria … you switched the damn thing on. That's wonderful … yes, sure, Sunday afternoon. She's lying on the same finger as me. G2, across and further in from me … well, you'll see her. Name's not very big, but she's a ketch, the biggest one in that row of biggies …*Pssst!*. I told you … yeah, pretty stupid. But you haven't met the owner … precisely. See you then."

Carlotta had made no mention of Harky, so Aria was surprised to find him sitting at the saloon table drinking beer with Ted and Carlotta. Somehow Harky even managed to give a certain formality to a nod and a sheepish grin. He had aged, but he still looked strong and his face was very tanned.

Ted was asking Harky about his sailing experience, as he looked up at Aria and patted the sofa beside him. She slid in but kept her distance. Ted raised his eyebrows at her.

"I need time, Ted."

He nodded and turned back to the conversation. To Aria's surprise, there was a good deal more to Harky's sailing years before he came down to Auckland where he anchored next to Carlotta. Then, as he put it, he was waylaid by a vegetable plot and Carlotta helped him sell his boat.

"Man, you've had some adventures!" Ted slapped the table. "And you, Carlodda. Are you Polish? You're an ocean sailor too?"

"I'm American and my granddaddy was Italian. Those guys on Ellis Island weren't hired for their spellin' skills, ya' know. But yeah, I've done blue water stuff. I hijacked a sweet little yawl outta Chicago. People I crewed for on the Lake were taking her down to Florida. Permanently. They got completely ready to go, then held a humongous party at the yacht club. They fell aboard and slept past leavin' time so I just cast off and did the sailin'. They woke up darn near into the Saint Lawrence Seaway." She put the emphasis on Saint. Ted was laughing uproariously. Carlotta kept her voice dry; she must have told this story many times. "Turned out I was a great heavy weather sailor, their best navigator … they kept me on and I convinced them they should just keep going while the money lasted. Florida would always be there. Of course, you then go right round, 'cos what else can you do with no money?" She was being deliberately droll, playing up to him.

Harky gazed at her with admiration. "Really! You never told me exactly … you *usually* went to a party with your *seabag and passport*? No. Well, that's … premeditated piracy?" He looked at Aria. "Is there such a thing?"

"There is now; Carlotta's set the precedent."

Carlotta was on a roll. "Well, it all went well—they were great sailors by the time I jumped ship in Tonga and grabbed another berth down here. They are still sailing outta Stuart, Florida. The Bahamas, Exumas. They're pretty old now."

Ted tilted his head. "And you're not? You must have a few years on me …"

"I'm fifty. That's hardly geriatric. I'll be still sailing when I'm seventy, you see if …"

"Well, if you're leaving port then, I'm coming too," Harky grinned. "I'm up for it, the voyage of the gerries!"

Ted leant back with his arms behind his head. "What about being on for this one, *before* you're geriwhatsit? Orya could do with spreading the load …"

"Stop. Ted, we've been through this. You can't just give me crew. I've got Carlotta and Oscar who are very capable. It's enough. Sorry, Harky, but …" She looked at Harky and saw his face fall; the dog that didn't get through the gate. But he seemed so much older than Carlotta, probably grew and smoked dope for all she knew, and hadn't sailed for a long time even if what he'd done before had been remarkable. No, he was not crew material.

Ted lunged forward, stood up and Aria moved quickly to let him shuffle round the aft end of the table. "I'm going. You sort it out. I'll be back later to lock up. Come to think of it, Cap'n Ma'am, you can."

He tossed her a key with a busty plastic mermaid attached by purple string. "Fine with me if you let Harky join you."

That makes it awkward for me, Aria fumed to herself. She watched him reach the far end of the pier. "Let's drink the idiot's beer." She raided the refrigerator. The yacht did not yet have the stove installed properly, but it had a large refrigerator for drinks. "Booze. Ted's one of *those*, I think, a marina sailor."

"Fanny, is he what! But he's not going, we are. Cheers!" Carlotta raised her bottle. "I got the seal of approval from a turkey."

"You could come whether you got his approval or not."

They drank beer for a while. "When are you taking her out? Soon?" Harky asked.

"I don't know. I'll figure what she needs first and get any work done. She's got a few basic instruments; for sea trials, she has the essentials. The compass'll be useless; its brain will be addled by the ship and need to be swung. We can use a hand bearing." She thought for a moment. "You know, maybe we should make that soon, before we all get fond of the idea and then find out she's a pig."

"While I'm here, Aria. Let me see if I'm still handy on deck." Harky looked like a puppy again, this time determined to get through the gate.

Aria laughed. "Alright. Next weekend, if that's okay with Ted. I'll tell Oscar".

Chapter Nine

Oscar was asked to a party on a Wednesday night. His mother looked sorrowful after dinner when he said he was going out. "Oh, you're not thinking of tomorrow. It might be the day you're asked to do something extra special at work and it would be wonderful to do it well."

He kissed her hair and said, "Get real, Mum," and she smiled. When he got there, he was bored by the conversations, his mind still on the planned delivery, so he went to the kitchen for water and left via the back door and the neighbour's fence. Risky stuff, if you are Samoan. At home, he sat with his parents watching the news and then told them the plan for the voyage. They were not surprised; he had been going to night school to get his Coastal and Oceangoing Yacht Master certificates. Oscar had thought they'd be alarmed. "It's no big deal, work-wise. I'll be away a fortnight, three weeks, a month maybe."

"Son, don't mess your career up for it but … aw, I wish I was sailing with you. I wouldn't go to Fiji. I'd hijack the ship to Savai'i, of course. What do you say, Lulu'a?"

"Sure. Hijack and pray." She dodged a cushion.

Oscar wondered yet again how his parents had kept this streak of childishness through thirty-something years of marriage. But they were cool with his plan. Only once had they not supported him wholeheartedly—when he switched majors to philosophy during his rugby, beer and band phase. He went off to bed grateful that they still believed in him.

***

Pssst!'s new sails were heavy and not very flexible. They rolled out neatly, but did not like the wind; they sat flat and hard. *Pssst!* felt as if she was resisting forward movement. They all agreed that it was difficult to say if she sailed well enough. She was quite true even with the flatboard sails, a little tender, and shipped a bit of spray in a sea. Harky shrugged. "You work with what you have. She'll get you fit either way."

Aria left the wheel to Carlotta and spent her time looking for problems; the shrouds and stays should be checked for even tension, the forestay looked light for the height of the mast, someone had forgotten a gybe-preventer. As she expected, the compass needed swinging. Below, she made lists of the items she thought could be useful.

***

On Saturday, when Oscar went down to *Pssst!*, he saw people sitting in the cockpit on Aria's little yacht. It was closed up. He bounded over. "Hey, can I help you? I'm Oscar. I work on one of the boats. You waiting for the owner?"

The girl jumped up. "Oh, you're Oscar? I'm Bree, Aria's sister. I've been dying to meet you since Aria told me about you." She was smiling broadly and leaned over to put a hand on his shoulder and kiss his cheek, ignoring his look of surprise. "I'm waiting to ask Aria to show me the yacht she's going to deliver—*you're* going to deliver. Can you show me? Us? Oh, this is my … this is Manny."

Oscar nodded at Manny. Unlikely bloke for Bree, he thought. Handsome but heaps older than her. "Come over. I'm just going to open up. There's nothing much inside, but you can see what she's like. I have to go back for a few things but I won't be long." They crossed to *Pssst!* and Oscar slid back the hatch and opened the slatted doors. "Open the forward hatch for a breeze. Back soon."

When he got back, Bree was already snoozing in the cockpit, sunning her long pale legs. Oscar sat down opposite, putting a stack of tools in boxes beside him. "What do you think? Okay? Aria says so and I believe she knows." He was aware of Manny's quick glance as he pulled cushions forward, lifted settee seats, peered into the lockers below and ran his hands round inside. Oscar wondered what he was looking for; it was an empty boat, apart from some food and galley gear.

Bree looked up at him. The top-knot was a bit much, she thought, but he had a pleasant strong face. "It's pretty. Looks safer, being so huge. Aria's is *crazy* small!"

"Aria's boat is a few feet over half the length, which makes it *much* smaller in volume. But I think you underestimate both your sister and her little Herreshof." His voice was gentle; he remembered Aria using the word 'frail' for Bree. "Aria's a cunning old sea-dog. Just doesn't look like one." He leaned towards the hatchway and called down, "Manny, you found any leaks yet?"

Manny's face appeared at the companionway. "I am interested in the woodwork. It has a cupboard or shelf everywhere. Everywhere!"

"It has, eh. That's how all yachts are. At sea, you can't have wasted space. And all areas of the hull have to be accessible, in case of damage. So yep, everything opens. What, you never been on a boat before?" Oscar squinted in the bright light.

"Oh, yeah. Big ones that motor, and ships. Many times."

"How was that? Your job?"

But Manny was not to be drawn. "I would really like to see this ship when she is ready for sea. Very different, I think?"

"No different at all, just stacked to the gunwales with gear. You'll be welcome to come down when she's readying."

But even as he said welcome, Oscar knew that he didn't feel comfortable with Manny. He resigned himself to putting up with him as Aria's sister's boyfriend.

Manny came up to the cockpit and settled himself by Bree. He asked, in a lazy way interspersed with chat and remarks to Bree, what the owner's plans were, then where she would be chartered in Fiji, if charters go as far as other island groups, whether yachts are inspected by officials in outlying islands, whether Aria would oversee everything loaded aboard ...

Odd questions, Oscar thought, answering as best he could and wondering why Manny cared. He watched them leave. They looked like two strangers who happened to be going the same way.

****

Later, when Aria came down to *Trinkitat*, Oscar strolled over. "I met little sister Bree today, and Manny. They came down to see if *Pssst!* looks like a real yacht, good enough for big sis. Manny opened every locker and hatch and even ran his hands around inside. What's with the guy? Said he was interested in the woodwork and how there's no wasted space. But you don't need to check every locker to work that out."

"Well, I've done it myself, to establish she's all properly built and safe. Must, if I'm to take responsibility for the thing. Ah, but you know, Manny's from another planet! He latched onto Bree when she was still a schoolgirl. Dad told him to ... clear off, quite a few times. We didn't see him for a while— maybe a year or more—but he reappeared big time when Dad was sick. He'd always kept in touch, I gather, and I guess he knew we wouldn't say anything to upset Dad when he was already so miserable. So Dad never knew it had all started up again. Poor old Bree, so beautiful, so smart, with such crap taste in men!"

"He's a funny guy. Asks questions no one else would ask, almost like looking for gossip, sometimes. What's his job?"

"IT. I don't know what he does, specifically. But he's not a gossip really—he doesn't repeat stuff. He's more a sticky-beak. Has to know everything about everybody and minds everyone's business to the last degree. He seems unaware he's annoying people—just carries on. I think he's just socially lacking or dysfunctional. Sociopathic, maybe. He should have been a detective or an investigative journalist."

"Hah! You take no prisoners, eh."

***

Well before Christmas, Aria had completed lists of gear to be bought from the chandlers to get *Pssst!* ready, and had a schedule of work requiring tradesmen.

Ted looked at it in dramatic dismay. "Orya! Orrrya!! That's going to cost a fortune! Replace some rigging because you think it's a bit light? It's the standard for this design." He threw himself back against the dark green settee, arms wide, in a gesture of expansiveness and generosity. "What gives you the notion my resources are infinite?"

They were sitting aboard *Pssst!*. Ted had knocked on her cabin roof but she had not invited him aboard *Trink*. "I'll be over!" she had shouted.

What a git, she thought now. He's hoping I'm aware of his wealth. He probably thinks money's the main attraction for women. "There are only necessities on the list, Ted. This is not the Kon-Tiki expedition; we need to be able to do more than drift with the current if things go wrong. Maybe cut down a bit on the electronics. I'm not into that stuff and would have to learn to use it; I should, I suppose."

"Well, give me the list. I'll ask my good friend Gerry over in Poor Street and see what he suggests. Some stuff might have to be second hand."

"Second hand is fine; how it works is what counts. Everything needs to be in good working order and more than able to last the distance." And after that, she thought, what do I care?

He was running rapidly down the list. "If you get this communication gear, why do you want a barometer? Isn't a weather forecast good enough?"

"No. The gear can break down, the forecast can be wrong, too general, out of date … there are lots of slips with weather forecasts."

His eyes crinkled into a laugh.

Aria carried on. "The weather warnings for the '79 Fastnet Race were too vague, too late, on a radio frequency that no one listens to … whatever, the yachts failed to get timely warning. A barometer never lies. Read it every hour, observe the wind direction and strength and you have the true story."

"Now is that so? And they shoulda just counted on their barometers?" His amusement spread to his voice.

"It would have told them a lot. Either some yachts didn't carry one or the skipper didn't watch it. A few of the yacht crews said it gave them the clue to turn back but … the rest? They could have known something big was coming. They'd still have taken a hiding, maybe, but as it was, a lot kept sailing right into it. The inquiry looked at just about everything else, but there's only one mention of barometers."

"Haha! You've read the report and based on your analysis of this ancient Fassnet, we need … a *barometer*!" He shouted with laughter, slapping the saloon table.

She waited.

"You gonna have a barometer, Captain Ma'am. Inscribed 'in memory of the '79 Fassnet disaster'. Oh boy oh boy!" He was breathless with glee and did not notice that she sat unsmiling, waiting for him to settle down.

She said doggedly, "I wouldn't even do a coastal trip without a barometer. It's an essential."

"Okay, okay. You'll have one. Gerry can run with the lists. Over Christmas New Year, I'll start getting *Pssst!* sorted out. Install the *barometer*, maybe, and get some of the small jobs done. Hard to get workmen to do much, this time of year." He shrugged. "But done, Ma'am."

"And she needs a sensible name. Something easy."

"Hey, where's your sense of humour? It's as sensible as any name I can come up with." He laughed.

"It's ridiculous, and won't be heard clearly over the radio. Something short and clear with hard consonants th …"

"Nope! No change, Captain Ma'am."

Aria watched him leave with relief. He had copied the Captain Ma'am thing from Carlotta, and she hoped it was not to go on too long. Carlotta was one thing, Ted another.

***

At Christmas, Aria set aside all work on the *Pssst!* project to sail Harky to Whitianga on her own little yacht. But back in Auckland, she found Ted had done nothing. There was no evidence he had been aboard. She said aloud, "Huh! Not that interested in his boat."

Chapter Ten

Aria stood open-mouthed. "Whaaat? You spent time with *Ted* this week? Ted *Halaby*? How do you even know him? That's just *weird*!" She stared at Bree, demanding an answer.

Bree shrugged and turned to her sink. "Oh, you know, it was nothing … Manny got tickets for a concert, and then he had to be away for a while so he gave them to Ted to go with me. Big deal." She was tidying an already tidy bench.

"So Manny and Ted are such great buddies that Manny hands over his girlfriend? You have to be kidding! If Manny has tickets for you both he can't use, how about he gives them to *you*, and *you* decide who to go with? Eh? Might that not be more normal? I know Manny knows of Ted, but this is definitely a bit strange."

"It's not, Aria, it's nothing. I just said to Manny that before you do this delivery thing, I hoped I'd meet Ted. And then when … well, it was just so I'd get to know him and feel better about you going."

Aria snorted. "Gawd, Bree. Ted's irrelevant. He's not going. Spend time with Oscar, he's the one going. Damn Ted. He's an obnoxious so and so; not the sort of person I want to bring into your life. Manny is an interfering idiot—and he's manipulative. So what else did you do with Mr Big? Eh?"

Bree's voice was small. "We had dessert after the concert, that's all. And the next day we went out to Waiheke on the ferry and swam and walked. He's nice, Aria. I don't know what you've got against him. He's lonely. On two days, I got called in for urgent work, two very long days, so he picked me up afterwards and took me to dinner."

"So you saw him just about every day."

"Um … yes, every day. I'm taking him to Jena's New Year's, I have to say thanks somehow, Aria."

Aria's voice was just below furious. "Yeah, well just make sure it's not the usual thanks. That's what he'll expect."

Suddenly Bree was yelling. "You mind your own business! You're not my mother! You don't know anything about my life! You always assume the worst about me without …"

"Bree, stop. I'm not assuming the worst about you. I just feel that this guy is a user, a schemer … I don't know. And Manny's no better. I wish they'd both clear off—out of your life. You know lots of nice men. Why can't you go out with them? Jena's brothers, I don't know … the tennis club, work … find someone new, Bree, not one of these dodgy damn types."

Bree looked pensive. "All the guys I know are so young. They talk about rugby or 'Varsity or IT or—oh worst drag— drinking. They're boring, childish. I guess I prefer men older." She tried to smile. "At least they're not married."

"That's what *you* think. I'll bet neither of those two feels any obligation to be honest with you."

Bree made a small sound, and Aria felt a stab of guilt; she had, after all, been away over Christmas.

"Oh Bree, I'm sorry. I've got to go, but I'm sorry—and for going away, too. It wasn't fair of me. Ted … I just have a bad gut feeling." She stepped out of Bree's front door and shouted over her shoulder, "And I still want to know how Manny knows Ted so well. Find out, will you?"

Bree watched her walking down the path to her car. She had wanted to say, "Arz, it isn't me or Manny or boats Ted's interested in, it's you," but she had not dared.

***

When January recovered from New Year, Ted called Aria. She had finally given him her mobile number. "Orya! How ore ya? Haha! ... Fantastic. Hey listen, about the electronics. I got a bead on a deal in Fiji. Guy's imported a whole system to refit his boat after going on a reef, and now he's decided to quit and sell the repaired hull bare. It's a fancy system that would suit my boat fine for chartering—all the new stuff. I've made him an offer close to new price. Now, where would that leave us for delivering her?"

"I don't need much, Ted. I'm a real sailor."

"Woho, hold on, I never said ..."

"Just listen. I have my own sextant. You just need to get a good quality spare—no point in a cheapo. I'll make you a short list. I'm not big on radio. I like being out of touch."

"Orya, *I* won't like it. That's my beautiful baby you're gonna be sailing. I gotta be in touch. Umm, a satellite phone ... yep! A sat phone. Righty-o, as they say here."

It was the one thing she had planned to buy for her single-handed passage and use on this one. "Ted, I'll buy one. It'd be useful on *Trink*." She laughed to herself at the thought of turning up in Suva Harbour without even VHF. Everyone but *everyone* had VHF, and it might even be a requirement. But she would be happy enough to sail in unannounced. "I'll get my own." She heard him starting to insist. "'Bye."

***

In March, *Pssst!* was slipped at Half Moon Bay and work on her became intensive. A stronger-gauge forestay was fitted, the sails

93

were softened, the tensioning of the shrouds checked and adjusted. Below, the plastic did not come off the stove; instead, the whole gas unit was changed out for kerosene because Aria insisted it was safer.

"Kero? Aviation fuel? How'm I gonna get a charter cook to use *that*?" Ted shook his head as if he thought Aria daft.

"Just don't take a cook on unless they can. No problem in Fiji; they're practical people. And if you're using Crewbay or something, just stipulate kero stove experience."

***

Manny did look over *Pssst!* again. Aria spotted him coming across the hard at Half Moon Bay heading towards *Pssst!*. She had been up on another yacht looking at its modifications when she saw him, so she scrambled down and stood on the bottom rung of her ladder, blocking him. "G'day Manny. What brings you here?"

"Oh, Aria, hi. The … my boss's boat is supposed to be coming out. I think he just wants to confirm when they lift it."

"Really. He probably could've phoned."

"How's *Pssst!* coming on? Can I see what they've done?"

Aria almost laughed. She wondered if his boss even had a boat. "Come on up." She bounced up ahead of him, curious to see what he was interested in. "Not a lot of changes inside. New stove, though." She busied herself in the cockpit and let him go below alone. And there he was, poking around, looking up under the cupboards below the new stove, upending himself to peer down into the bilges below the engine, pushing and pulling at things.

She could see what Oscar meant. Manny-the-sticky-beak was searching, and she needed to look harder herself. She did, but found nothing.

***

Aria and Oscar went sailing together nearly every weekend on *Pssst!,* once she was back in the water and ready. Ted said he was coming a couple of times but did not turn up. In late March, Harky arrived and he and Carlotta both came sailing if she was not working and *Chicago Gal* did not need watching. Aria and Carlotta barely moved from the cockpit when they were out. Harky and Oscar did almost all the deck work on *Pssst!*. They began calling each other Bro and Uce in an exaggerated way. Carlotta rolled her eyes. "Is Oscar the real deal? Surely he knows that's not the right use of the term."

"It's cute. They really like each other, and Oscar's making him feel welcome." Aria smiled. "They work well together. Going to be different at sea, though. We'll all have to do our bit."

Aria asked them to use her Dad's special code to alert her from the cockpit. "I'll hear it amongst the other noises. He trained me, like a sheep dog. He called it D, though it's a bit of a stretch to relate it to Morse." She rapped on the cockpit seat. Tap. Taptap.

"Okay. Good and loud might do the trick," Oscar grinned. "And I'll try yelling when it doesn't work, eh."

Aria smiled. "It'll work. I always wondered, did Pavlov's dog have a name?"

"There were lots of them. One was called Chenghis Khan." His rumbling laugh threatened to start but he kept a straight face.

Chapter Eleven

And then it was *that* day.

Aria had *Pssst!* ready and had been watching the weather patterns. She saw that they would have a three-to-four day fine spell of good, though strengthening, winds, which would see them well north of New Zealand and any land hazards. She had given her 'advance notice of departure' three days before, and *Pssst!* lay briefly at Z pier in Westhaven Marina, cleaned up, watered up, fuelled up and stowed. It was a big boat, but somehow, it was full. Ted had stocked it with far too many books, without asking what they liked to read. They all added their own anyway. That was Ted; he just assumed he was right, she thought, and said "Huh!" loudly. Oscar's parents, chatting with the crowd of friends gathering beside *Pssst!*, looked at her with surprise. She smiled. "Just a thought."

Harky sat on the cabin top with his back to the mast, calmly whittling a small figurine. Whether he was doing it for dramatic effect the others did not know, but it amused and delighted the little crowd.

Aria left Bree and her friends and went below where Oscar was stowing more food that his parents' friends had brought.

Ted wore fashionable nautical clothes and sat importantly at the table drinking beer with Manny. The manual for Aria's new satellite phone lay in front of him. It was an Oceana 800 and he had been explaining its range and use to Manny, who looked bored. "Sit down with Orya and me a moment, Oscar. We'll just check these lists again. Orya, you picked a great li'l baby, here." He stroked the manual.

Aria's mouth pulled into a moue; Ted was making a show of checking that all was ready while they lay, cleared, at Z pier! "I think it's the one for the job, Ted. If it isn't, it's a bit late."

Oscar's eyes narrowed a fraction at Ted. "Of course the lists are done, Ted. We'll have forgotten stuff, but we forgot it before the lists, eh. Aria, let's just throw the lines off and get out of here. My parents are going to start praying soon."

Aria clapped her hands. "All visitors ashore." Ted and Manny obediently got up and went back up to the pier. It was a week morning but even so, there was a good turnout. Mat had come, and gave her a one-armed squeeze around the shoulders, perhaps all he dared. "Safe journey, my darling," he whispered.

She murmured, "Thank you."

Sure enough, Oscar's father lifted his arms to get attention and his sonorous voice drowned everyone out. "Let us pray for those going to sea, that all come safely home." He repeated it in Samoan. It sounded like magic. The Samoans led the way and everyone stopped their chatter, bowed their heads and listened. Harky stopped whittling and stood in a thin litter of wood-shavings. Rev. Niu proceeded to ask God to bless those who braved the sea and take care of them bodily and spiritually and to…" In the background of the prayer, two little girls sang something mournful in high sweet voices.

Aria whispered to Oscar, "Bit spooky, isn't it?" but he shook his head and mouthed, "Normal."

Rev. Niu had barely intoned "Amen," when Carlotta breathed, "Fanny!" and then loudly, "Thank you, Reverend!"

There followed a frenzy of hugging and kissing and wishing well and Harky swept up his wood shavings and disappeared below; he had no one to see him off. Manny had moved further away to take photographs. Mat stood behind Bree with his arms around her. As the three crew stepped aboard, the Samoan church ladies sang a haunting song of farewell. Tears sprang to Aria's eyes. Oscar laughed and said, "That's me that's supposed to crack up. Hey, cheer up. It's going to be fun." He put out an arm to her but she dodged it.

"I'm just excited and happy and touched at your family's way of doing things. I'm fine." She stepped behind the wheel. "All good, Harky?" she called down to him. And to Oscar and Carlotta, "Cast off." She started the engine.

***

It was like leaving Auckland on any trip up to Whangarei or the Bay of Islands, but under their ribs there was a huge contained excitement. Cape Rodney to port, Little Barrier to starboard, far ahead the Hen and Chickens and the Mokohinau Islands, and almost due north, Fiji. Clear of the channel, Oscar had a sensation of stepping into the abyss and at the same time, the glorious feeling of freedom that is the gift of the sea to all sailors.

***

Out beyond the Hauraki gulf, *Pssst!* felt the ocean swell and her movement changed. They had a good breeze from the west and skimmed through the seas on an easy beam reach. Further out to lee, a giant cruise ship towered against the horizon, a city block that had slid off firm ground. The wind smelled clean and cool, and for a few hours, all sat on deck in silence. Finally, Harky went below and set out Samoan treats.

As soon as they were out of sight of land, Oscar brought out his camera and took photos of the sea and sky.

"What? You know what that will look like, don't you?"

"Well, I just want to record what it's like when there's nothing anywhere." He ignored Aria's laughter and held out his camera.

"That's not nothing; there's a ship."

He scanned the horizon, brought his eyes back to one point and grunted agreement.

Aria had jotted down a schedule of watches: Carlotta and Harky on together from six until ten, morning and evening, including making breakfast and dinner, Oscar ten until two, Aria two until six preceded by making lunch. No one argued for the early morning watch, which surprised Aria. She had thought both Harky and Carlotta would know its delights. It was her favourite, and even galley duty and the long afternoon, the other half of the watch, were not enough to put her off.

Carlotta, she knew, could do anything on board reliably, except perhaps up-mast work; Harky was still a bit of an unknown so she has been happy to give him shared shifts and let him contribute through cooking and the myriad other little jobs that fill the days at sea.

Below, things were joggling into place. They had stowed carefully, because they all knew it is not what you have but how you look after it that is important.

By early afternoon, all were yawning and went below but it was Aria's watch. She settled down with the self-steering working strongly, keeping a watch on wind and waves and other vessels. Nothing much changed, and the rhythmic motion and rush of water under the keel almost made her nod off sitting up. But she was too wary a sailor for that and drank tea, called for dolphins, "Te Puhi!" and made her hourly recordings until there was stirring below just before six. The sinking sun lit the high cloud in hues of red and orange. Not quite red but shepherds' delight. She had heard Oscar's friend, Jonno, saying, "Red sky at night, won't rain. But it might!"

Oscar slept on until they woke him for dinner. He's young enough to be able to sleep whenever and wherever he pleases, Aria thought. She'd had to teach herself to sleep when she had the opportunity, and now could just lie down and drift off. As a single-hander she had to be able to do it. She remembered Carlotta's comment, "Big kid," but had felt it just applied to Oscar's enjoyment of life. She was confident he would take his job seriously.

The cool of evening slowly overtook them and they were glad of hot food. "Harky, this is wonderful. If you do two meals a day, I'll absolve you of all other duties."

He laughed. "Carlotta had it ready before we left. But I'm more than happy to do the rest. I learned to sail in Canada—that's good for toughening you up, and hot food's important. I continued when I was at school in England and carried on from there. I've sailed on and off all my life, since I was about eight. Katie, my beautiful wife, was a Kiwi and she sailed too. Then when … my life capsized and some friends readied their yacht and were setting off for South Africa, I quit and begged a berth. They said if I cooked two meals a day … well, I've come full circle."

All but Aria put on more clothes and stayed on deck until Oscar's watch. Late at night, they sailed towards a strip of bright lights from Asian squid boats, dotted from horizon to horizon.

"Fanny, will you look at that! It's like a highway in the sea." Carlotta decided not to call Aria up because, when they were closer, they saw that the ships were widely spaced.

Eventually the squid boats were a distant necklace of lights. Oscar swung down the companionway and retrieved his guitar from the roof of his cabin where it was held by firm bungy cord.

"Oh boy! The accompaniment for the massed choir of the *Pissed?*" Carlotta laughed.

Oscar softly sang, *"In the night, the warm night …"*

Aria lay tucked into her bunk with the lee cloth up, roused occasionally by their singing or laughter, and each time drifted off again with the joyous feeling of being at sea.

***

Tap. Taptap. Oscar woke Aria at 2.30am. She came out, looked at the chronometer and scowled. "It's half an hour into my watch. Why didn't you wake me at two?"

"You just looked so peaceful. Beautiful moonlight night, eh. I don't feel tired anyway, too excited and too afraid I'll miss something. There are dolphins everywhere, seems like."

"Well, you'll miss a whole lot more if you fall off your perch. You keep your watches strictly to time, and if you can't sleep, lie in your bunk and think happy thoughts so at least you rest. We'll be exhausted by the unaccustomed movement in a day or two and I want everyone to be on deck if needed. Who knows what happens next?"

Within ten minutes of handing over, Oscar was fast asleep tucked into the angle of a settee. When Aria jumped down to have another quick look at the chart, she saw that he smiled in his sleep. He threw his arms up to whack against the bulkhead, groaned and brought them down again but the smile did not fade.

Aria looked again at Oscar's entries in the log. According to the figures, they were slipping along at seven knots but a bit to the west of their course. It felt good with the wind and waves just slightly forward of the beam. On deck, she shone her torch up the sails, looking for anything untoward. They were pulling well and *Pssst!* felt happy enough. She loved the cold wind in her hair but knew that she would soon be too cold. She reached below for a woolly hat, and pulled the hood of her oilskin over it. High up just inside by the companionway there was a little rounded shelf with woolly hats (communal), sunscreen, a tube of lanolin, small binoculars, a scrunch-up sunhat, socks (also communal) and another torch.

Above her, the few swishes of mares' tails had thickened up and obscured the stars here and there. The moon was just disappearing over the western horizon; soon it would be only intermittent starlight. She shone her torch up on the vane at the masthead; the wind was backing and strengthening slowly. She eased the sheets slightly to bring *Pssst!* back onto their planned course. *Pssst!* changed her movement quite noticeably and Aria heard some mutterings from below. The little kerosene lamp on the forward bulkhead bobbed and swung to a pitch and roll.

By 0400 hours, the wind was steady at eighteen knots, and *Pssst!* was tearing along. Aria felt, as she often did at that hour, that the wind and waves were more aggressive, that things were not far short of out of control, but her recordings showed that all was well. She remembered the Christina Rosetti poem: "*There are sleeping dreams and waking dreams; what seems is not always as it seems.*" That pre-dawn hour always did a bit of seeming and not seeming.

Apart from its diurnal dip, the barometer held steady. It was very dark, now that the moon was down. She scanned the sea and horizon constantly, sometimes thinking her eye had caught something dancing. She remembered her father's technique of looking just beside where you thought you saw it, but there was nothing.

Occasionally, dolphins squeaked as they came rushing up and played by the cockpit. She did not know whether some played in the bow wave or not. She had a firm rule that no one went out of the cockpit alone on watch. The dolphins amused her, or themselves, for a while and sped off and she saw to starboard that the sky was lightening in the east.

Aria watched the lovely sunrise, thinking of other dawns, of sailing down from Noumea, of running over the hills behind the milkers with the frost on the grass, of her mother up before dawn cooking porridge or bubble-and-squeak, and of Mat. Damned Mat, who had loved dawn too.

Silver preceded gold, gold faded back to silver, then gave way to blue once the sun was up. Before she had time to fill in the log, Carlotta bounced up on deck for her watch, throwing her arms up, calling "Good morning! Oh, Princess, was there *ever* such a morning?"

Aria's face was lit up like the sky.

***

On the second day out, Oscar woke at daylight with Carlotta and Harky and shared their watch. Carlotta looked at the chronometer when breakfast was done. "Oscar, you could go back for another few hours' sleep. We're fine—we don't need any help. I'll do this and Harky can stand watch."

"I'm good. I'll keep Harky company for a bit."

The wind strengthened steadily, and relentlessly built the swell and waves. Harky was happy to be above deck, too, and to have company.

"You been back to Norway, Harky? You still got family there?"

"Loads in Norway, though I've lost touch a lot lately. All round Bergen. After my father retired from the diplomatic service, my parents moved close to wherever I was. They wanted to be near us once I was married to my beautiful Katie and we got Arun, our son." He gazed out, his eyes seeing something else. "Arun was adopted. We found him when we were on a hiking holiday in the Karakorams. He … he'd been abandoned and an old man was feeding him. He was about two, we thought, incredibly thin but beautiful, with skin like honey and blue-grey eyes." Harky's voice was soft and slow. "Katie wouldn't leave him. He became tremendously attached to her— he needed a mother. She stayed on in Pakistan and after a dreadful struggle, we managed to adopt him. I'm ashamed to say that in the end we used my father's diplomatic pull to get it through, and of course now I wonder if it would've been better not to."

Oscar reached for the glasses and identified a ship on the horizon. It was overhauling them on a parallel course. He put them down and looked at Harky.

Harky sat slumped against the coaming then seemed to gather himself to sit straighter. "But my family. My mother passed away while we were in Paris. They are both gone now, Father a few years after Mother. My oldest brother took him home to Bergen when he needed to be looked after. Wonder if I'll dement like him? Little by little he lost it over those years in Paris. It was vascular, the medical people said; a little accident here, a little accident there, in the small vessels of the brain. But my brothers are older than me, and hale and hearty, as the English say. Maybe we'll all last longer and better than our father."

"Don't you want to go home to see them, then, or go back to live in Norway and be near your brothers?" Oscar wondered about his wife and child but sensed that he should not ask.

"Yes and no. I lived all over the place as a kid and young man, only about a quarter of it in Norway. But I've always thought of myself as Norwegian. Still do, in spite of my Kiwi passport. Once you emigrate, you never really settle in the new place but you can't go back to the old one, because it isn't there anymore. Terrible thing, emigration. The whole darned world's on the move at present, and what they don't know, most of them, is that they might *have* more where they're going but their loss will be enormous."

"You think so? My parents came from Samoa and seem perfectly happy in New Zealand."

"Well, perhaps they did it for the right reasons in the first place. I did it to escape my memories; only partly for the adventure of sailing off with those crazies and coming to New Zealand to help Katie's father." He gave a rueful-sounding laugh. "It's healthier to go for a positive reason in the new place than a negative one in your homeland. You see what I mean? But unhappy people emigrate. Emigrants are more likely to have depression or be nutters; I've studied it because I am one—an emigrant, I mean." He grinned.

Oscar observed Harky's face. He had flashes of amusement and even joy, Oscar thought, but they faded fast. He seemed at least happier at sea than he had in Auckland.

Carlotta was singing at the galley bench, strapped in. Aria was sleeping through it.

"Yeah, my parents talk about Samoa constantly, and sent me back every holiday to keep my links with the place. Nearly died of happiness when I got my pe'a, our traditional Samoan tattoo, but I don't think they'll ever go back to live there. Too involved with what they're doing in the Samoan community in Auckland and perfectly happy where they are."

"But they've family there?"

"Oh loads, eh. But we aren't quite part of it. Well, we are, in that you'd never notice any difference, but we were kind of adopted by another family. Dad's main attachment is to the church, though. Did I tell you the story of my family? When World War I broke out and the NZ Expeditionary Force took over in Samoa, Germany sent two battle ships, the *Scharnhorst* and the *Gneisenau*."

Harky nodded. "Ah, yes, of course."

"They came, they saw, they sailed away, really. But they caused a lot of excitement. My—I don't know—great grandmother, I suppose, maybe great-great, was out on a canoe watching the ships sail off and she swam for a coconut. But it wasn't a coconut, it was a head." Oscar's rumbling laugh erupted. "It was some German sailor off the *Gneisenau*. They rescued him as the ships left. The Kiwis locked him up for quite a long time, and when he got out, old Oscar, he married her, and for some reason took her to live on Savai'i, where the 'Sisus adopted them into their family. That's why we're called Niu—

coconut, haha! He dropped his German surname; I don't think anyone now knows what our real name should be. S'pose I could find out through the records of the Kiwi occupation, but we like Niu." He was still grinning.

"The Pacific Islands! There's nowhere like it. Well, NZ has been very kind to me, and every day, I put my feet where my lovely Katie put hers and our little Arun played." Harky smiled his wonky sad smile. "But it's good your family are happy and settled. Leaving your country is usually a very sad thing."

Chapter Twelve

On the evening watch, after Aria went down to her cabin, Harky amused them with a Norwegian sea shanty.

"It sounds like the Sesame Street Swedish cook got a job on the Picton ferry," Oscar said. He left his precious guitar on the saloon roof and brought the ukelele out of his cabin. He carefully picked a spot in the cockpit, safe from spray. Then he tucked the ridiculously small instrument against his body and picked up the chords as Harky sang Dibdin's ditty, learned from his English shipmates.

One night came on a hurricane,
The sea was mountains rolling,
When Barney Buntline slewed his quid,
And said to Billy Bowling:
'A strong nor-wester's blowing, Bill;
Hark! don't ye hear it roar, now?
Lord help 'em, how I pities them
Unhappy folks on shore now! ...

On it went. Aria half heard the laughter on deck as she lay tucked into her odd athwartships berth, feet lower than her body, and wondered if a sudden rogue wave might reverse things and throw her on her head. The bunk was only good for a night with a lover in a calm little harbour. She abandoned it, shifted to the berth aft of the galley and was soon asleep.

***

By the fourth morning, the seas were rough and the wind stronger. It had veered to the south, and they had changed course slightly to take it on the starboard quarter. *Pssst!* was rolling more. Oscar climbed out early and joined the others for breakfast. When Carlotta went below to begin her routine of early morning tasks and Aria was settled in the quarter berth, Oscar and Harky sat in the cockpit together. Oscar scanned the horizon and took photographs of empty sea or cloudy skies.

Harky gazed fixedly astern, his face drawn and tired. "We did a lot of sailing, Katie and I, from Lymington, on the same yacht I sailed out to Australia. They were a good bunch. And Katie was a good sailor. Her father taught her. She swam like a fish and had the most incredible resistance to cold water. I'm a Norwegian but she beat me. Well, our waters are so cold we try not to get wet. I don't swim at all in Norway. But when we lived in Spain it was different. We swam, sailed … young Arun was a natural sportsman. And cricket! I think it was in his genes. I had to learn to play, after all those years of avoiding it in England." He grinned briefly and looked into the distance across the waves.

Oscar gazed over the ever-shifting scene and wondered again where his wife and son were now.

Harky brought his eyes back to Oscar. "You mind if I reminisce?" He did not wait for an answer "We met in London, Katie and I. We were both at LSE. I was doing a degree in maths and economics, and she did geography and economics, with an honours year in EU policy planning. She was a smart girl. Smarter than me." His face lit with happiness at the memory of that time.

Oscar murmured, "Good years, eh?"

"We did many things. She was a good all-rounder; she climbed, sailed, rode horses. Our first years together were in

London, then four years in Paris, and finally … finally five years in M … in Spain."

Oscar nodded and waited. There was something coming.

"We had gone to Paris by the time we got Arun. His name was Aryan but it didn't seem like a good idea, so we just changed it that bit. We got him a Kiwi passport, so it wouldn't have mattered too much, I suppose. Paris was fun for us but restrictive for a child. We were glad when I got a transfer to Spain and Katie easily wangled another job there with the EU lot."

Harky abruptly got up, went below, made tea and put it on the cockpit floor. "Carlotta's in her bunk reading. You want to go down for a bit before your watch?"

Oscar shook his head. "No, I'm good for smoko."

Harky clambered up again. "I'm glad you're here. Thanks." He left his tea on the floor of the cockpit and took a deep breath. "You see … in Madrid, everything came to a halt. When they went … when they … it was like the world stopped and there was nothing. Stillness and silence forever."

Oscar wondered what 'went' might mean. After a moment, he made a gentle sound that had something of a question in it. Harky stared at the horizon for a long time, and when his voice came back, it was tight and low. "They were in the restaurant—we stopped at a restaurant—the one that was bombed in '95. I was … parking the car."

Oscar was so astonished he stopped breathing. He had not imagined that this was the sort of thing Harky had been through. There was a long silence while Oscar felt as though he had lost the ability to speak. His throat went so tight that when he tried, he made only a soft humming sound.

"That was the end for me." Harky's voice dropped to a harsh whisper. "Only it wasn't." He drank his tea.

Oscar put his still half-full mug down on the floor. He tested his voice. "They were both …? What did you do?"

Harky was silent and slowly finished the tea. "I walked. I walked north to the start of the Pilgrim Way, and then I followed the trail to Santiago de Compostela. I didn't speak to anyone the whole way; I had nothing to say. It took me many weeks. When I sat in the cathedral, I realised that it was just as hard for Katie's Dad and I went to New Zealand to see him. He was done. It was horrible for him, and horrible to see him like that, too. He wouldn't come back with me; he wanted me to stay."

"You didn't?" Oscar hoped it did not sound critical.

Harky forced a deep breath. "I couldn't, not then. I went back to sort things out, but for three days I just sat in our apartment in Madrid, stunned that they weren't there. A Spanish colleague came round and got hold of me. "Come with me," he said, "Just come." He took me to a concert, a chamber orchestra playing Paganini and Boccherini, and it was that that started a change. It reminded me that there is also human excellence."

Oscar seemed to be struck by the words and was silent for a few moments, staring at Harky's face. "Human excellence. It was music that helped you find that?"

"It was the crux. My brothers were kind. They kept in touch but let me be. After that, I went to see them. I couldn't face Katie's friends; I felt ... I dreaded them asking questions, and worse, feeling sorry for me. I couldn't explain my presence, why I was still around. I drove myself crazy with questions. I used to go over and over it. There were no answers. Why did Arun say, "This one. Let's stop here."? Why did I drop them in front and not take them to the car park with me? Why did we think he was better off with us? How could the bombers *kill a child*? I just couldn't understand any of it. I still can't."

After a long pause, Oscar spoke gently. "No sense can be made of people doing those things. Except that they have lost their grip on reality."

"Perhaps." Harky studied his face without seeing him. "Yes, and lost their humanity." His eyes wandered to the horizon. "Sometimes I think we are so busy now trying to see everyone as equals that even fanatics and the downright criminal are acceptable. We've gone collectively soft in the head, I think".

Oscar nodded. After a while, he said, "But the music?"

"Oh, everywhere, I looked for concerts." He tried to smile but it was a grimace. "Live performances of Mendelssohn, Albeniz, Sarasate … anything. It was to hear musicians play—see their effort, their skill, their dedication to creating something momentarily beautiful for people they will never know." He gazed out, seeing something else, his face softening. "The will to create an exquisite gift for an unknown other; *that* is what it is to be truly human."

Chapter Thirteen

As time and the strong wind went on, all four worked harder and struggled more with the pitch and roll. Oscar put a deep reef in the main, and both it and the much-reduced jib pulled hard. They were cutting along with a very wet deck.

Aria kept a close eye on the barometer readings and reassured them. "It's nothing much, really, just a good strong airflow. It will ease off eventually. Then we'll be sorry, like as not. But in the meantime, all hands observe the rules carefully— no accidents, ok? Make sure you're still in good order when it blows itself out."

Now she always slept in the quarter berth by the galley. She had the lee cloth up, but did not lie against it. She used an old sailor's trick; she lay on her side, facing uphill, her top knee pulled up with her leg under the squab, her upper arm forced under it too and held by the weight of her head. No matter how rough it might get, she slept securely.

Oscar was surprised when she came up for her 0200 hours watch, bright and enthusiastic. "You slept in this? I don't think I will. Too rough and jerky."

She told him how and he looked sceptical. "Yeah, well, maybe. I'll make some tea for us both, then I'll try it, eh. Doesn't sound likely to work, but I'll give it a go."

He brought tea and biscuits, wrote the log, and sat with her gazing over the wild rough water for a while.

"Oscar, rough or not, you have to sleep."

"You going to be ok? Call me if there's anything to do. G' night." He got up reluctantly.

"Take the quarter berth. Still warm. Up forward is rougher. Maybe Harky should have taken yours. He's close to exhausted. And yes, I'll give you a good hard D if I need you. We must have two on deck to do *anything* in this. Good night."

She did not see him again, and when she dropped below to grab a snack at three, she could see in the dull light a tangle of gleaming oiled hair, one huge shoulder and a thigh-length of his pe'a in the quarter berth, his lower leg hidden by the squab.

* * *

Harky and Carlotta lost their balance a couple of times and Harky began to look haggard, Carlotta worried. On day five *Pssst!* was thundering along when Aria called Carlotta up at daylight to bring her course round slightly to make the movement easier. Aria began making breakfast as Harky scrambled up to go on watch with Carlotta.

"No need, Aria. I'll be down soon; just reviewing things with the officer of the watch," Harky called down the companionway, in a lively voice. Carlotta laughed. He clung hard to the sissy bar and said to Carlotta, "Why did I give this up to be a subsistence farmer in the wops?"

She snorted. "You're dumb, that's why. But you're wisin' up." Harky chuckled. Carlotta knew that he had gone to live with his lonely old father-in-law and later inherited the farm that would have been his wife's.

When Aria handed up plates of eggs and bacon, Harky looked a lot less bright and lively than he sounded. She made toast. "Oscar," she whispered, "You want breakfast?"

There was no reply. Oscar's breathing was gentle and slow. His head was thrown back and that absurd smile lay on his lips again. She watched him for a moment before she put the toast on the cockpit floor.

On deck with her own breakfast, she looked at Harky moving cautiously and realised that although he had just rested, he was pretty done. She wondered if she should have said no to his coming, but a glance at his face, drawn but bright, made her think it was, at least for him, a happy choice. She was glad the wind was dropping.

He saw her concern. "Hard work, this bit of a blow, but worth the effort for an old beggar like me. But there'll be no voyage of the gerries, Carlotta. I think this might be my last dance with the wild wide sea. '*How can we know the dancer from the dance?*' Eh?"

Aria's mouth dropped slightly open. "Yeats. How does a Norwegian know Yeats? Oscar's a poetry freak too. You never know what you've got, Dad used to say, 'til you put 'em in a shearing shed or take 'em out to sea."

"Oh, everyone who had an English education knows Yeats." He laughed. "'*Those images that yet / Fresh images beget / That dolphin-torn, that gong-tormented sea.*'"

Carlotta snorted. "Poetry! Fanny! What the hell is a 'gong-tormented sea'? *Gong?*"

Harky shrugged. "Who knows? It sounds good, Carlotta. Yeats was a mystical poet—slightly crazy and magical. '*And therefore I have sailed the seas and come / To the holy city of Byzantium.*' There is a vessel astern, starb'd quarter horizon."

"On the starboard quarter on the *gong-tormented* goddam sea!" Carlotta was still shaking her head. "Fanny! The guy was nuts alright."

Aria carried on into Carlotta and Harky's watch. Harky was clearly tired, his eyelids drooping, and he went gratefully back to his bunk.

Carlotta's face showed concern too, and she tidied things that did not need tidying. "Your watch schedule is all to hell. You happy up here, I'll get cookin' ahead. Now the wind's droppin', it will feel rougher; no one'll be cookin' and then we're done for." She strapped herself into the galley to port, and sang,

"Cookin' ain't kissin'
But it go less fast,
Yeah, kissin' more fun
But it cookin' that last"

but she sang it quietly. Harky and Oscar slept.

Aria stayed on with Carlotta, enjoying the fresh wind blowing her hair over her face, and the vigorous sea which always fascinated her. On the starboard horizon, a merchant vessel slid by. At the end of Carlotta's watch, she tapped D on the cockpit coaming. Tap. Taptap. Tap. Taptap. She heard Oscar's deep rumbling laugh, and he emerged shirtless and tousled for his 10 am watch, his topknot unravelling. "Warmed up at last. How far have we gone?" He leaned over the chart. "We're flying!" He pulled the band out, combed his hair with his fingers and tied his hair up again in a bigger mess than ever.

"Yep. Position marked there is pretty good." Carlotta indicated the chart table with a wave of a spatula. "We're nearly halfway, and averagin' seven. Course good, cookin' even better."

Oscar sniffed. "Mmm."

"You missed breakfast; it's morning tea. Harky likes all these *teas*." Carlotta grinned; they both thought the term quaint. She handed a plate of pancakes across to him. They were running with butter.

"Hey, you're no galley cook. This is Queen Street tucker, eh. I thought maybe ships biscuits and a bit of spoiling cheese." Oscar took the rest of the pancakes up into the cockpit, with honey, jam, Marmite and tea, and laid them on the floor. He held Aria's mug out to her. "Good morning, Captain."

Aria sat in the cockpit, smiling eyes crinkled, ever watchful. Her face was flushed or sunburned, lips peeling slightly, but her eyes very blue and bright. "G'morning, Oscar. Did you look at the chart? Great run, eh? But the wind's still dropping. It's fading out quite quickly now. Pity. We might have the inevitable calm upon us soon."

"Mm-hmm." He was tucking into the pancakes, his lips glistening with honey.

"But it'll be easier for Harky. He's been quoting poetry this morning—Yeats, no less."

"Nn know hum." He gave his lips a thorough licking to unstick them. "*That is no country for old men …*' can't remember any more. That was Yeats, wasn't it?"

Carlotta gave a derisive laugh from the galley. "That's just seagullin'. Everybody knows that! It was the title of that movie. Yeats! *Gong-tormented*!" She went to wake Harky for tea and pancakes. "Hey, nap's over, Harky! I got morning tea ready. Morning *tea* … Harky? *Harky?*"

He did not wake.

Chapter Fourteen

Fear gripped Carlotta's throat and made her voice rasp. She called Harky's name again, but there was only a flicker of response. She tried her nursing tricks and slapped his cheeks, dabbed his face with a wet cloth, lifted his eyelids. His eyes did not focus on her. She felt his pulse, irregular and slow, leaned close to his face and felt his breath on her cheek, a bit *too* deep, a bit *too* slow.

"Harky, wake up, you have to drink water." She hauled him up on one shoulder and arm and took the plastic tumbler from the gimballed holder. She felt him try to help as he drank in little sips, losing a lot. Then his eyes drifted shut and she could not stop him falling back.

Carlotta got out the medical kit and took his temperature in his ear. Normal. She opened his mouth; his tongue lolled to one side and she had to push it in to close his mouth. "Harky! Oh, Harky!" There was no response this time, but he was still breathing. She left him and ran through the saloon. From the companionway, she called, "Aria?" with her voice tight in her throat. Aria heard her fear.

"Watch things, Oscar." She jumped below. "What is it, Carlotta? Harky? Where is he?"

"I think he's had a stroke, Aria. I can't wake him."

"Oh, Carlotta … d'you know what to do? We'll have to act fast."

"I should have given him aspirin while I could; now I prob'ly can't. We'll have to get help."

In the forward cabin, Aria stared at Harky's slack face in horror. Carlotta lifted his free arm a few inches; it fell too heavily and he did not stir. She lifted his eyelids. His eyes looked back at her unseeing. "I think he's extending, fast."

"Extending?"

"That's what they call it when a stroke gets worse—greater area of damage. He needs treatment *now*, really, to stop it."

"Oh God." The sat phone was calling. Aria ignored it. "This is not something we can deal with, is it."

"No, there's nothing we can do, Aria, except care for him." Carlotta sponged Harky's face, her own cheeks wet with tears. "Aria, we need to call for a ship to take him off. I don't know if it will help him any; what can a ship's doctor do, at sea? Oh but they'd manage his fluids and get to port faster than us. We'll be another four or five days, won't we?"

Aria nodded. "Yes, four. But this wind won't keep up much longer. The barometer is rising a bit so it'll tail off. Might leave us with nothing, now we're getting into the tropics. I'll put out a pan pan. I saw three ships on my watch, and there'll be more we haven't seen. And I was given the contact details of RCC when we cleared out." She knew she was babbling from fear. Carlotta must have known that RCC was the rescue centre because she did not ask.

Aria called up to Oscar that Harky was unconscious, and she was going to call for assistance. The sat phone was calling again. Ted. She cut it off, and jotted down the coordinates of their last position in large figures, called the New Zealand Rescue Coordination Centre and asked them to put out a pan.

*****

Within minutes, several ships responded. The nearest was heading for Sydney, but her captain said she was an old freighter, probably too slow even if she diverted to Suva or Nuku'alofa. The one which passed them hours earlier was the *Aloysius Glory*, Panamanian registered, from who knows where. She was a tanker, under ballast, having discharged at Marsden Point. They could make good time, they would effect a transfer, her captain told Aria in what sounded like rehearsed English phrases. Her captain agreed to come back, made arrangements to verify position when closer and ensured they could communicate with each other. Aria struggled with his very strong accent, repeating what he said when she understood it. She closed off and called to Carlotta, "You keep up with that?"

"Yep. Not gonna be easy. But I think we have to do it."

"Carlotta … tell me if I can help you. Or call Oscar, if you need lift him."

Oscar was bringing the sheets in more as the wind backed and abated. The motion was less comfortable because the seas were still big. They were keeping their course, slightly west of a direct line to Suva because Aria, although scrupulously careful about navigation, had a greenhorn's nervousness about reefs on the Tonga Ridge. Once they were past the latitude of Minerva, she would allow more easting to bring them into Suva. Oscar had independently calculated a morning position, and his differed very slightly. It mattered; they needed a noon sight to be sure of their position.

Aria's worried face appeared in the hatchway. "Oscar, Harky's in bad shape. Carlotta thinks he's had a stroke."

"How crook is he, Aria?"

"Bad, she thinks, and getting worse. He's completely unconscious now, but just before, he drank some water, so that's something. A ship's coming to take him off ..."

Oscar's voice was calm. "I heard you talking on the phone. You know how to do it?" She was shaking her head at him as he carried on. "I've read about transfers at sea. It mostly depends on the conditions at the time. You get the ship to hold station, side on to the wind so that you can lie in her lee, and you hold your position if you can. You put out bunches of fenders if you go alongside, but even so you're likely to damage the rigging."

Aria was staring at him, wide-eyed.

"If it was calm seas, it'd be easier. But they might put a boat out, or send their medical officer over. I guess we see what their Captain suggests at the time."

The sat phone was beeping. It was the *Aloysius Glory*, steaming for them. The captain wanted to know more about the 'injured seaman'. Carlotta prompted Aria as she struggled to explain. "He has had a stroke ... a brain clot or... yes, like a brain injury ... Oh, no doctor? Crew with first-aid training. Oh. Listen, can your first aider ... what, Lotta? ... give him fluids by drip? Ok, that might be all we can do. Ok. Yes. Listen, we are not a ship, we are a yacht. Small, fourteen metres ... *Pssst!* ... yes, like pissed. Yes, we will confirm position again soon."

The sat phone called again. The New Zealand Rescue Coordination Centre said that a New Zealand naval vessel was making for the Western Pacific, currently south of their position, slightly more distant than the *Aloysius Glory*. She could reach them in three to four hours if they hove to. It was the *Canterbury*; they had trained medical officers and facilities to deal with all emergencies. Aria felt tears of relief pricking her eyes. She was worried about the time lapse, but the *Aloysius Glory* would not have been any faster. This was a much better option.

She called the *Aloysius Glory*, told them and thanked them. The captain's voice was lighter. "OK! We don't do this thing before. We please to help but more please now you have good luck." The *Canterbury* called and gave Aria instructions for communicating.

Aria flew up the companionway. "Oscar, we are going to heave to. We're waiting for the *Canterbury* now. It's one of our navy ships, don't know what sort, frigate maybe. We'll organise *Pssst!* and then I'll go down for a rest until she's nearing us. They'll be three to four hours, they say. That ok with you?"

"Yeah, but I don't know much about heaving to, eh. You tell me, I'll do it. However we do it, let's do it gently—we don't want to throw Harky about, I reckon. I've adjusted things a bit. The wind has gone right round to a straight easterly, now, right on the beam. That's why the waves are a mess."

"We're going to bring her round hard onto the wind and sheet everything in—yeah, I better warn Carlotta—and then without releasing the jib sheet, point her to windward, so the jib backs. Then we'll lash the wheel so she's trying to come up all the time. That's supposed to hold her. I've done it on *Trink*, but I don't know if every yacht does it the same. Maybe not."

"We can do that, I reckon."

She ran through the saloon to Carlotta. "We're going to try to heave to. Let's wedge Harky in tight with clothes or squabs or something. Then you just hang onto things until we get sorted." They pushed anything they could find under the sides of the squab, steadied his head and Carlotta tightened up the lee cloth.

Aria ran her eyes over it, nodded at Carlotta and dashed back to the cockpit. "Oscar, I'll bring her up and haul in the main. You sheet in the jib good and tight."

Aria disconnected the self-steering and slowly brought *Pssst!* up hard onto the wind, hauling the main in as Oscar brought in the jib. *Pssst!* heeled and surged forward, and then as she went across the wind, the jib backed with a thwack and *Pssst!* stalled, falling off a bit. Aria held the wheel over to push her bows to windward and Oscar lashed it in place with the end of the mainsheet. *Pssst!* lay about sixty degrees off the wind, heading south south-east, making a short jogging motion combined with an occasional roll over a bigger wave. She continually pulled up and fell off, but it was not much. Aria and Oscar sat in the cockpit watching for half an hour.

Oscar nodded and grinned. "So we're satisfactorily hove to, eh? Seems okay, but we're pointing the wrong way. If we were going, we'd be going home."

"We won't. We'll drift a bit; west, I think."

Oscar nodded. "I can't believe how it takes the busyness out of her. It's positively peaceful. Hey, you got a problem with that left arm?"

There was a slight hesitation and Aria turned away. "I had an operation year before last. Had tough rehab and couldn't sail for a while, then I got started again on gentle days. Now … pretty much anything, I think. I'm just careful of it. I wouldn't absolutely trust it with a sudden hard force above my head because it hasn't quite got full movement. Nearly there, though."

"Did you have a tendon repair? My rugby bro, Rudey, had to have that, after he tore it nearly through. They said he'll prob'ly never get the last few degrees, never get it right up again."

"No, no damage. It wasn't the shoulder … I …" Aria waved a hand at the rigging. "Looks ok, eh? You sure you're alright for a bit? I'll go and rest so my wits are about me, and I'll keep one ear on the sat phone. You'll do our position again, at noon? That's important."

He nodded. "I'm good. Strange not going the way we're headed. You have a rest and I'll sit here watching her."

"The drift's inevitable. We'll find out." Aria dropped below, and found Carlotta constantly busy with Harky. She dripped tiny amounts of water into his mouth, sponged his face, checked that the towel that she had tucked between his legs was not too wet, all the time whispering assurances and endearments.

Aria stared at the sat phone. I'm glad I've got that phone, she thought. But she had no sooner lain on the settee nearest the navigation table than the phone disturbed her again and she snatched it up. Ted.

"Orya! What the hell? Five days and you don't call in? You some kinda independence freak? You tell me don't-call-me-I'll-call-you and you don't for five days? Listen, I can't get…"

Aria talked quickly. "Ted, I'd have called you if there was anything to report. We are on a great run, about half way, in biggish seas, wind dropping, so we are damn busy! But *Pssst!*'s fine."

"Orya, listen! I can't get a flight to Fiji for a while. Can you slow down? Drop a few…"

Fear turned to fury. "No, I bloody *can't* slow down and I won't try. We'll get there when we get there and you do the same." She cut off. Half her head was wondering why she didn't tell him what had happened, and half her head knew. She checked on Carlotta, lay on the settee closest to the navigation table, and listened to the sounds of the yacht. Hearing nothing untoward, she let herself drift off.

Chapter Fifteen

Aria woke after two hours, immediately thinking about the impending rendezvous. She jumped up. *Pssst!* seemed to be less comfortable, keeping up a jogging motion with a twist to it, pitching and rolling occasionally. "Carlotta, it's two-thirty. What's happening about the *Canterbury*?"

"We've spoken to them twice. Fanny! You were out cold! Oscar did the log and checked our position. The wind's fallin' off and the sea's still rough. Slightly west, we think, of our original position. They're on track. They estimate they'll reach us in a bit over an hour. Bit late in the day, but it'll have to do." She added softly, "Harky's no different, except maybe his breathing is weaker. He's not taking any water in. Boy, I'll be glad when they get him on board."

Aria was halfway up the companionway. "You're doing your best, Carlotta; it's all you can do." She leant down and gave her half a hug. On deck, it was a messy scene. The waves were still occasionally breaking, the swell not as big but shorter and the wind was not holding *Pssst!* so well against the waves. She was joggling and twisting about like a puppy resisting its first lead. "Hey, Oscar, how is it?"

Oscar flicked his head sideways. "This is strange, doing nothing with all this happening. Oh, except the log. I've kept that and done a noon shot. We've drifted a couple of miles, according to my reckoning. You have a sleep? Ready for this next bit?" He was scanning the horizon ahead over the starboard bow.

"Have to be. We'll let them tell us what to do." Aria pulled a face and dropped down beside him. "What a thing to happen."

"Yeah, poor old Harky. Even worse for Carlotta, really. Well, he was having a great time. He loved it."

"I know, but I should have realised that it was getting too much for him. He's not old, you know, only looks it. Carlotta says he's in his late forties. We could've hove to yesterday, or the night before. I just thought it was all the falling about you do when you first go out, getting your legs. Thought he was tired, not unwell. Carlotta doesn't know whether it's a bleed or a clot, but she says a clot's more likely. Statistically, for all the help that is! She says she is pretty sure he hasn't hit his head."

"Dad's always on about this stuff. Live each day as if it's your last … blahdiblah. *He* might, but nobody else. Well, maybe Harky was. You never think of anything happening, eh?"

"No, but things do ... especially at sea."

They sat together for a while until Oscar noticed the waves were becoming smaller. "It's settling down."

Aria's voice had an edge of sadness. "Dad just ignored his symptoms for a start. If he'd said anything, we'd have made sure he saw a doctor. Maybe that's why he didn't, I don't know. But he had secondaries before he was even diagnosed. He only lived seven months, and in that time I had my operation, and Mat left soon after Dad died. Well, he didn't leave. He just made it impossible to go on. Yep, bad luck can slug you and go on slugging."

"Woe, you had a hell of a time. Your husband … Mat? Are you divorced? He quit when you were going through all that?"

"Well, it was eighteen months or so altogether. No, we're not divorced—but we will. He doesn't want to, but I'm *sure*." She pulled a strand of salty hair away from her eyes and grimaced.

"He had a bromance. It's the affair men have when they're not having an affair, y'know? I could have got past it at another time, maybe, but it was having it at that particular point, when I needed him so much. Dad was dying, I didn't know how I'd come out of … it was an awful time and … he hardly talked to me. Hopeless bloody… oh I don't know what."

Oscar laughed. "You don't often swear, I can tell. But you're alright now, aren't you? You seem only *mildly* bitter and twisted." He looked at her from the corners of his crinkled eyes.

"Haha! I'm not sure whether it's mild or not. Some days it all seems pretty raw, but I suppose I'm getting over it all. Bree is still very needy. She has been, really, ever since Mum died, and my problems and Dad going capped it. I wish she'd meet someone *nice*. She knows heaps of nice guys and chooses hopeless ones like Manny. And Ted. *Ted*, for God's sake."

"What? Ted? But when we left Auckland, I didn't see her say more than hi to him. They an item?"

"I don't know. Manny engineered it; he gave them some tickets. And Ted took it on. You know how Ted fancies himself attractive to women. Manny plays games and no one ever makes sense of what he's up to. I'm so fed up with him. I wish he'd leave Bree alone but not by handing her over to bloody Ted as if she's a parcel."

Oscar said gently, "It's her life, Aria. She'll figure it out. You just need to re-ravel yours."

"I know. Thought I was." She jumped up and scanned the horizon. "I suppose Carlotta will go with him. I should get their papers sorted. Don't know what they need."

"Passports for sure."

"Their passports, umm … copy of our crew list with yacht's details. What else, do you think?" She had multiple copies of the crew list. She swung down the companionway and looked up for his answer.

"Dunno. Anything you think they could possibly need. Oh, their bookings for flying home. But the crew'll tell us." He stood clutching the sissy bar and scanning the horizon. "Not a thing in sight yet."

***

Aria had been helping Carlotta with Harky when Oscar shouted below, "Ship bearing almost due south. Only just on the horizon. Can't see any gadgetry aloft …" and then almost immediately, "… Oh, some … but maybe not the *Canterbury*—funny looking thing—container ship, probably. The swell's a lot bigger than it seems but I'll tell you when it shows above the sea again."

"OK." Aria called back and hugged Carlotta. "This might be them, Lotta. Let's just see how it goes, but be slow and careful. Yes? Here, let me help you."

Carlotta had fanned a folded towel between Harky's legs and needed to keep it in place as she put his tracksuit pants on. They smelled of urine. She had hauled them off and dried them out because he had only brought one pair.

Aria wrinkled her nose and Carlotta laughed. Together they managed it. Carlotta smoothed Harky's hair and murmured, "We're getting' you a better berth real soon, honey. Gonna get you fixed up just fine, navy style."

Oscar shouted down, "It does look like it's them. There's a bunch of gadgets on top. Could be her, I think, but I can't really tell."

Aria took the sat phone and called the *Canterbury*. "Yacht *Pssst!*. We see you due south, we think. We are hove to. Can you give a position, please?" She jotted it down, gave her position and compared it with theirs. It was almost certainly the *Canterbury*. "You have us on radar? *And* can see us. Yes, we have white topsides and sails and an NZ red ensign … yes. No, we don't have VHF. Ah … yes, just the sat phone. Okay. Readying for you."

On deck, Aria and Oscar caught more and more frequent glimpses of the ship, then watched her grow larger. She was a strange looking vessel, shaped more like a bulky cargo ship than a fighting machine, with a vast open aft deck. In the bright sunlight she looked white not grey.

"Oh, I wonder if we do have the right vessel. Just doesn't look likely. I never noticed anything like her at Devonport." Aria dropped below and called them again. They assured her that they had the yacht in sight, hove to, at approximately the coordinates she gave. Aria dashed up again. "They seem to think they know who we are."

"And they think we know who they are?" Oscar grinned.

She laughed nervously. "Let's hope so. Oh, now that she's closer, I think I have seen her before. I didn't know what she was. Okay, we'll just follow their lead."

Aria felt impatient. The *Canterbury* slowed down well before the approach. She steamed carefully and sedately towards them, but she was a cumbersome-looking craft. Aria went below again to the sat phone. She was instructed to change nothing, to stay hove to and they would put out a tender. She told Carlotta who said that Harky was about as ready to jump ship as any guy had ever been. Aria flew up the companionway. The *Canterbury* lay a couple of cables off, directly to windward, and a flurry of uniformed crew were readying a rigid hull inflatable boat on deck. It was swung over on davits. Their ship was rolling slightly, but the boat landed neatly and evenly on the water.

Aria held her hand to her face. "Oh gosh, it's huge—looks half as long as we are! Well, a bit of overkill might be good in these seas. Oscar, I wonder how we'll get him up on deck? Could you carry him?"

"Probably; he's a skinny old coot but I don't think they'll need us. They'd have told you. They'll have the gear for moving him."

The big rubber boat came bouncing and jostling alongside, and Aria estimated that it was indeed about half the length of *Pssst!*.

The crew tethered her fore and aft to *Pssst!*'s suddenly-little cleats, and they bucked and rolled together.

An officer swung nimbly up saying, "Aboard … Aria! You name this thing?"

"Sophie Garrett! Oh wow! I did know you'd joined the navy but …"

"Lieutenant Garrett, now. Haha! I wondered about that name, Stihl. I can't believe it." She turned to Oscar. "We haven't seen each other in—oh, twelve or more years. We were at Auckland Girls' together. And you're crew?"

"Yes, I'm Oscar Niu." He answered, turning to help receive the space-age equivalent of a stretcher.

Sophie's eyes lingered a moment on Oscar and came back to Aria. "Right. Let's get on with this."

Several more of the *Canterbury* crew climbed aboard with the doctor, leaving two men in the RHIB. Aria stepped out of the way, and spoke quickly. "He's in the forward cabin. He's in very poor shape—unconscious and floppy as a sleeping baby. He's been like that five or six hours now, we're not sure. He seemed to be tired and just sank into it, in his sleep. Got worse fast, and we haven't been able to do anything for him. Not even give him water, now. Please be careful with him," and to Sophie, "Can his partner Carlotta go with him, Sophie? She's a nurse; she could help with his care. And she'll just be fretting with us."

Sophie smiled. "We don't need any help, but she can come. It will be good to have someone with him who can answer questions, fill in some detail, keep him company."

It took only a few minutes for the doctor to check Harky, nod with pursed lips and tell Carlotta that they would put a drip in immediately they had him safely aboard. The crew were ready with the narrow stretcher, a kind of foam sandwich arrangement that held him cosily. They carried him high through the saloon, and Carlotta said, "All good, Harky. They could float ya' down the Nile in that." He was raised carefully up the companionway and out on deck.

Oscar bent towards him. "See you in Suva, old mate."

Sophie threw an arm and a fleeting glance at Oscar. "Make way. please."

Aria slipped down the companionway. "Here, Carlotta, you're going with him; you'll be able to help him. This is some of Ted's money. Grab your sea bag and some clothes and stuff. We'll deliver the rest wherever you end up. Sophie has both your passports, a copy of our crew list and the printout of your flight bookings. I don't know what else you need; they haven't said."

Carlotta snatched up a few clothes, apparently randomly, and flung them into her sea bag. She grabbed toothbrushes, a cake of wet sea soap, Harky's comb and a hairbrush and threw them in amongst the clothes. "Fanny! I don't know what we'll need.

I'm just grabbing some stuff. I ain't done this all that often, ya know."

On deck, Sophie took their passports and the papers and flicked quickly through them. She put them in a waterproof folder and stuffed them into an inside pocket. "We'll proceed to Suva, Aria. There are medical facilities there that we've used before and you can rely on. It's not a lot longer than going to Nuku Alofa, and our doctor," inclining her head towards the medical officer, "will have your man in as good a condition as we can manage as soon as we have him aboard. We'll take good care of him."

"We're very grateful for all …"

Sophie barked instructions at the crew and they rigged a line to tether the stretcher, with Harky tightly swaddled into it, as they took it out and lowered it neatly into the tender. Aria was relieved to see that the crew seemed prepared for each toss and roll.

Carlotta threw her arms round Aria and hugged her. "You and Oscar keep safe, Princess. Take no risks. When you arrive there's not important, remember, so don't let Ted pressure you into taking chances, huh? We'll be watchin' for you, Harky and me." She gave a wry smile and blew Oscar a kiss. "Be seein' ya, world's best." She gave him a thumbs up and climbed down into the jostling RHIB.

Sophie dropped lightly into it after her. She grinned up at Aria. "It's great seeing you again, Aria, but not like this. You two'll manage her to Suva, I'm sure. No weather in the next few days. I see you've got all the gear, except comms." She shook her head. "Bit primitive, you know, just having a satellite phone. Anyway, good sailing!" The tender had been cast off and pushed away from *Pssst!* when Sophie shouted over her shoulder, "Hey Aria! Get a VHF!" Then, even louder, "And re-name that thing, will you?"

Chapter Sixteen

Oscar wiped his forehead with the back of his hand and dragged it across his shorts. "Can you believe it? Just like that! I thought it was going to be an ordeal and we'd have damage or injuries or both. Awesome!"

They watched as the whole boat, crew and all, were lifted onto the deck with the speed and ease of landing a fish. Aria shook her head. "That was impressive efficiency. I made myself sleep but I couldn't help catastrophising again as soon as I was awake. They made it look easy. Well, let's get this boat sailing again; it will be dark soon. Not that … oh, eight knots of wind isn't going to take us anywhere fast." In the west, the sky had hints of red and gold on the scattered cumulus as a bright sun drifted down towards the horizon. Aria continued to watch the intense activity on the *Canterbury*'s deck which she assumed was Harky being lifted out of the tender. The ship was already moving off. "I hope they can start treating Harky. Carlotta says time is everything with strokes and it was a long wait."

Oscar frowned. "He *might* have hit his head, I suppose. But my impression was he only lost his balance a couple of times and banged himself about a bit. As we all have."

"Well, he's got a better chance now. I'm sure these … um … multi-purpose vessels have everything. I've read about the NZ Navy's one, I realise, just didn't know what she looked like.

She's more for humanitarian work, apparently. In this case, function is beauty." Aria laughed.

"Functional maybe, but it's ugly." Oscar gazed after it.

Aria watched the Canterbury gathering speed. "I should have hove to at least two days ago; this might not have happened. But it wasn't bothering *Pssst!* and I was enjoying it. Or maybe just shortened sail right down … though we might have rolled more. No, I should have hove to."

"Aria, don't beat yourself up. It wasn't necessarily the conditions or Harky's tiredness that caused it. Carlotta was tired too. It might just have been an accident that was going to happen. You know, I think Harky kind of knew?" Oscar squinted at her. "I dunno, maybe he didn't feel well, but I wonder if he felt his time was short or something was coming. He kept wanting to talk about his wife and son, and go over the dreadful time when he lost them. Almost as if it had to be done and done soon."

Aria raised her eyebrows. "I heard snatches of your conversations. Who knows?" She shook her head and stared out at the ship rapidly shrinking away.

"Pity he picked me to tell. I wasn't any use to him. I was so shocked I couldn't say anything. Wouldn't you think some of my father's skills with unhappy people would have rubbed off on me? But I was useless. Poor old Harky."

"Maybe it didn't matter what you said or didn't say. It wouldn't change anything. He might just have needed to tell it to someone who could understand, comprehend his pain. You're that person."

"Me? I've never lost anyone. It would be unbearable, I reckon. Harky's pretty amazing. He isn't angry, just can't understand it. Can't figure out how the sequence of events could have led to that."

The sun, now red, was on the horizon, throwing splashes of colour up onto the remaining rags of cloud. Oscar frowned up at the sails. "D'you think we should goose-wing?" The wind was almost a southerly again, and close to astern.

"No, we'll just roll. Bear off a bit, I think. We'll go nowhere much in this, anyway. You ever seen the green flash? Sailors are always looking for it. I think it's that thing where if you stare at a red light and then close your eyes you see green because there's a lack of red."

"I've heard of it, but this is my first ocean crossing, remember. Hah! Might be my last, after that." Oscar brought the jib round and sheeted it, then eased out the main. *Pssst!* responded and glided softly off again, on a broad beam reach. The *Canterbury* was only occasionally reappearing on the swell, away to the north.

Oscar gazed after it. "You know, I forgot to take a photo. I've got all these pictures of waves and clouds and ships on the horizon and then all that happened and I forgot."

"Photography born of boredom, maybe. No, I do know why you take the sea and sky." Aria smiled. "Oscar, you make us something quick to eat, and then sleep. You've been up here for, what …ten or eleven hours? I'll do right through 'til six. It's a bit of a mess but I've had a sleep and it will get our times straightened out. Then we'll do six on, six off, eh? You mornings and evenings, me afternoons and nights."

Oscar shook his head. "But we'll never see each other."

"No. Just in passing. That's how it is."

Oscar chopped cheese, tomato and cold sausages that Carlotta had cooked, and cut the last of the very stale bread.

Aria was amused. "What's this? Banger salad? That's imaginative." She realised they'd forgotten to have lunch.

"I'm a good cook, too, believe it or not. Had to help many times with the feed-the-multitudes thing. I just *like* cheese sandwiches."

Evening settled around them, and Oscar lingered on deck. The air was soft and warm and the trickle of water under the keel was almost like soft laughter. They felt as though they were only doing a few knots, but the wind was with them. The *Canterbury* was long over the horizon.

"Before you go, let me check the chart …" Aria jumped down the companionway. "Yes, we'll have the wind on our starboard side and get a better course for Suva. Don't really need westing now; our drift gave us some."

Oscar adjusted the sails and then gazed up at the rigging. "What a day. Once they suss what's wrong with Harky, surely they'll do more for him than just give him glucose and salt."

"Well …" Aria shrugged. "Wind's going to drop to nothing, I reckon." She, too, gazed up at the sails. "Yes. Incredible day. And Sophie Garrett!"

"Yes, what a woman, your Lieutenant Sophie! She knew her stuff, had her eye on everything."

"That was amazing. But I shouldn't be surprised. People carry on the way they start, you know. She was always the organised, reliable sort—sports captain, prefect, sound person. I don't think Dad socialised with her parents much—hard for single people to be included in the couples sets."

"You drop out of your couples set when you got … ?"

"Separated. But yes, to a large extent, soon as I started living alone again. It's like monkeys that get thrown out of the troop— hah! They're regarded with suspicion by the socially normal ones."

"Sophie was impressive alright. But you're like that. Did your Dad treat you like a son? Expect you to be capable and responsible like a boy?"

"What kind of a sexist remark is *that*?" Aria put a hand to her head. "Damn, that reminds me I haven't called up Ted. This might all be on the news. Oh to hell with it! I'll speak to him tomorrow. He'll find out. I'd better call Bree soon, though. She might be pretty alarmed."

"Yeah, the job of the press, now, is not so much to inform as to excite." Oscar laughed. "I'm not tired. Too much in one day, need to settle my mind. How about you sit down and tell me how come the cat was called Trinkitat? Just 'cos it rhymed?"

"I saw it in my school atlas. Yep, it rhymed." She laughed. "I was only eight. Seemed wildly witty at the time."

"Uhuh. Where was your farm?" He was gazing at her at close range, face impassive. "And why didn't you stay there?" She did not answer immediately and he wondered if he had been too nosey.

"King Country. There's a little place called Aria; I'm named after it. Locals thought that a good joke. It has about three streets. We left after Mum died when I was fourteen and Bree was five. Dad … I think it was all just too much, two kids and the farm, down in the King Country. So he sold it and got a job with the Wool Board up in Auckland. Office job, mainly, though he did go away sometimes and my aunt looked after us, the one who's in a home in Ashburton now. Better really, to move to town, and I needed a good high school." She nodded.

She's convincing herself of that, Oscar thought.

Aria gazed out over the port bow, turned away from him. "Not better for me though; I missed the farm. I used to wander all over it, spent whole days doing stuff like shifting sheep on my own. Trying to catch pukeko. It got me out of the house when Mum was sick, though I didn't know she wasn't going to survive it then. I didn't know what was wrong, just that life was too full of un-saids, full of *something* worth avoiding. I think that set me up for liking to be on my own at sea." Aria laughed. "And at home too. I like living by myself."

Oscar nodded but said nothing.

***

Aria called Bree, refused to let her butt in, and explained what had happened. She took it fairly calmly, for Bree, Aria thought.

It was a long night. At midnight, Aria splashed her face with cold water. She grabbed the thermos of tea Oscar had made her and was back on deck within a minute. She was still in the clothes she wore yesterday and maybe the day before. She glanced around and checked the anemometer. Six to eight knots of wind, not holding steady. The self-steering worked well in a good breeze, but this was not enough. She took the wheel. What wind there was now came from the south-south-east, and *Pssst!* was only ghosting along.

The moon was bright, the sky clear and full of stars. How fast things change, Aria thought. She remembered Charlie, her old navigation teacher, advising his class, in his dry way, of the dangers of alcohol at sea. "Sure, have a drink at sea. Get roaring drunk if you like. Why not, if you know what's going to happen next?" As usual, half the class had gasped and looked perplexed. When daylight had come yesterday, over much the same seas as the day before, she could not have imagined that Harky would lose consciousness, that they'd rendezvous with a naval vessel and have him taken off, that she'd meet up with an old school friend, that the wind would fall right off and the seas flatten out so fast, or that only she and Oscar would be completing the voyage. Not even a day and the whole picture was quite changed. She thought of Mat's old Māori adage: *Never turn your back on the sea.* Well, out here that might be the trouble; there's always a bit behind your back. She knew this was part of what she loved, that element of surprise that every day offered.

She had a few visits from dolphins, but apart from that, it was a peaceful night, the seas gentle, the wind never getting above eight knots, the flying fish somewhere else. She scanned the horizon, looked up over the sails, looked again behind and ahead. It was a dark night, so she did not nip below and grab her star chart, as she would usually. She settled down to drinking tea and being vigilant.

But waiting for the sky to lighten, Aria felt the familiar disquiet of that last hour before the dark sky softened in the east. She felt impatient with the wind and seas, suspicious of small sounds, anxious about Harky, guilty because she hadn't informed Ted, annoyed because Bree's calmness probably meant that her expectation of trouble was simply being confirmed. At last, the sky paled, turned silver and brightened the little puffs of dark cumulus above the horizon. Her worries began to melt.

Oscar appeared slightly earlier than six. He looked bright and well rested, and had combed his hair. Aria was glad to hand over. *Pssst!* was only just sliding along through the gentle sea, up and down the remaining swell with a bit of a roll.

"Good morning! Tea? Oranges? How was the marathon watch?"

"It wasn't so bad. I single-hand, remember. But I got antsy before daylight, as I so often do." Aria checked the log, and found they had travelled only forty-five miles on her watch. As she came down to mark the chart and make her recordings, Oscar took up Carlotta's cold pancakes spread with butter and golden syrup. *Pssst!*'s sails were barely filling. "There's more breeze than it seems; we're going with it." He watched the sails. "Put the spinnaker up?"

Aria came up to the cockpit and looked around. "You need a troop of gorillas on the foredeck for a spinnaker, really. We could motor sail."

"Let's try the spinnaker, eh? I don't like the engine, and I fancy myself a seagoing gorilla." Oscar was already down the companionway. He threw open the forward hatch, pulled himself up out of it, leaned down and dragged out the pale blue spinnaker bag. He forced it up through the hatch, and spilled it out onto the rolling foredeck, dropping the bag below and closing the hatch. Aria was impressed by his energy. He called back to her, "If this sets OK, I'll open that hatch and air Harky's cabin—smells a bit … um … piddlish."

Aria enjoyed watching him draw the spinnaker out to find tack, clew and head; he was fast and accurate. He took the lashing off the pole, fixed it to the lug on the mainmast, attached the sail and yelled, "You ready for this mess?"

She laughed when he hauled it up and it went aloft cleanly, flapping and filling as it gained height and ballooned out, full of wind. "Hey, you're more regatta rat than sea-going gorilla. It's fantastic—obscures half the sky from here." Aria listened to the renewed chuckle under the keel and looked behind at a straight wake. "I think we're using that tiny wind as efficiently as we can. What are we doing? Five knots—fantastic, in such a light breeze. Can you handle it now? It will collapse easily if things change. You'll have to steer." She took a last look around. "I'll call Ted. I might find out what his plans are."

Oscar nodded, took out his flute, steered with one foot and played.

Aria shook her head. "You'll come unstuck doing that—bit of an extra roll and the whole arrangement will tangle before you can correct." She nodded as he put one hand to the wheel and pocketed his flute.

Sitting at the navigation table with the sat phone, Aria winced at Ted's loud intrusive voice. "Orya, how'zit? You manage to slow down at all?"

"Yes, Ted, but not intentionally. The wind's abated, died, almost. …Yes, ghosting along but the spinnaker gear works. Oscar did it quite easily. Listen, you might have heard that the *Canterbury* took a sick crew member off a yacht. No? Well, it was us—Harky—and Carlotta's gone too … yesterday afternoon … well, I'm telling you *now!* … Yes, just Oscar and me … No, it's not *cosy!* We are pretty damn busy, doing six-hour watches."

On deck, Oscar smiled; Aria was shouting.

"Yes, everything is fine … how would I know what they said? Buy the papers. Read them. Watch the TV news, I don't know … okay, okay. Listen! We are fine, the boat is fine … Another four to five days, I'd say. I'll let you know if anything changes …yes. Bye."

She called Bree again and told her they were under sail again and doing well, and before she could call the *Canterbury*, they called her. It was not Sophie; it was one of the communications officers, probably. "Sailing yacht *Pssst!*. I am communicating an update from HMNZS *Canterbury*. I am sorry to give you this news, but crewman Haakon Paulsen who was evacuated from your yacht is still critical. Erm … our doctor … provisionally …" She was reading slowly. "Extensive brain damage caused by a clot or clots … erm, it says ISQ—I'm sorry, I'm not sure what that means. We are proceeding to Suva and will leave Ms Tedesky there to rejoin you. You will need to deal with the Fijian officials in relation to this but of course you will have consular help should you need it. … Yes, we have contacted them. I wish there was better news. … Yes, please keep in touch as you need."

Chapter Seventeen

The wind had almost died off when Aria woke at noon, refreshed and immediately alert to the quiet. The spinnaker must have been only just filling; she had to listen for the chuckle under the keel now, and there was only an occasional soft splash.

She brought Carlotta's soup to the boil and threw in some peas. "Food is going to be pretty hit and miss. Our fresh stuff is about gone, but there's Carlotta's stew."

"Wouldn't that be too old now?"

"No, it's in the pressure cooker with the trivet still on, so it'll be fine for days and days." She put the two mugs of soup on the cockpit floor and stood looking around. The sea was calm, with little wavelets dancing along to a feather-light south-easter. Occasionally a bigger wave slopped against the stern. *Pssst!* was barely moving over a gentle swell.

When Aria had sat down, Oscar raised his eyebrows at her. "All in order? Just? We'll need to watch the wind closely. Hey, tell me about bromances. I've been wondering if my friendships with my bros, like Jono and Rudey, are bromances or not? They both have girlfriends. I don't just now but we three do everything together. The women don't necessarily get priority."

"A friendship is a friendship. You know what that is. A bromance is an intense thing with another guy—the kind of obsessive state of being in love."

"In love with those smelly guys? Yeeuck! Never!"

"It's an emotional *affair* if you already have a partner, just as intense and absorbing as a sexual one—I daresay less complicated. But not less destructive."

"I can imagine."

Aria's voice was tight. "Mat had all the signs. He softened his voice when Grant rang, he turned away from me or left the room to talk. Talked for more than an hour, sometimes, even when he was supposed to be on call at the hospital. They'd have rung me, of course, if they couldn't get him, so it didn't really matter. Never turned down an invitation from Grant, even when things with Dad and my health were falling apart. They developed a special language and their own in-jokes—yep, a bromance is pretty intense compared with a friendship."

"Did they …? I mean …?

Aria laughed at his lack of words. "No, I don't believe they did. But it was the emotional desertion I couldn't take. He went on living with me but took his love away from me and gave it to this other person. It was hurtful."

"I bet it was. That's cruel."

"And when I said "That's it, I can't take any more," he seemed amazed that I saw it as anything more than just spending time with a mate. Even claimed he was giving me space to deal with my problems. He denied Grant was anyone special at all, denied that it was an affair—an emotional affair. Said he loved and supported me wholeheartedly. And you know, I think he was sincere. I think Mat truly lacked insight to that degree! That was the crunch, really, when I realized that he was a person who could *utterly* fool himself. I didn't respect him anymore. Well, to hell with him!"

Oscar looked out at the glinting sea, the faintest of smiles on his lips. A giant ship, well off, slid across the murky distance like a fast-moving slug. "Yeah, to hell with him. And on to Fiji with us."

Aria smiled, looking at the masthead again. He thought the skin on her neck very beautiful, stretched like that.

"What say we take the spinnaker down, Oscar, and I motor on my watch? Can you sleep with it roaring away? We might catch more wind: it should come in from the east up here. I'll motor sail if we get any. Let me check our position." She was thinking of reefs again. She jumped below and looked at Oscar's 1200 hours position.

They let the soup sit on the cockpit floor while Oscar brought the spinnaker down very cleanly, grinning widely at his success. "This spinnaker thing doesn't seem so bad. How does it screw up?"

"Hah! Let me count the ways! It's responsible for more foul language in racing than anything else. Foul language in voyaging is usually more to do with arriving ... ohhh, and blocked heads, self-steering problems, slipping engine belts, things falling with lids not properly on, stoves that won't light, hatches not properly closed by the crew... yep, more foul language in voyaging and cruising, I suppose."

They had travelled two and a half miles in the last hour. "That's miserable, but some motor-sailing'll be good for the batteries."

Oscar was peering at the horizon. "Looks like a ship with its bows falling off. I saw a picture, once, of a ship in Durban that had fallen off a square wave in the Aghulas current, and its whole bow was bent downward." He reached for his camera.

"Too far away." Aria fumbled for the binoculars, but Oscar had already enlarged his photograph to a grainy image of a ship with a gap in the stacked containers.

"Oof! I hope they didn't let a whole line of them slide into the sea!"

Aria started the engine, drew in main, furled the genoa and *Pssst!* slipped along over the calm seas at six knots. Oscar wolfed his soup, waited for Aria's mug and disappeared below. Aria set the self-steering and wrote up the log. She noted a couple of ships. Most took a leg northwest out of the Hauraki Gulf, then a straight line north towards Nadi before sailing east for Suva. This took them very wide of the Tonga seamount, well clear of the Minerva Reefs where the *Strathcona* had come to grief. Aria remembered it because their farm had been called Strathconan.

Chatting the long afternoon away with Oscar would have been nice, but she resigned herself to solitude. She picked up her book, *This Thing of Darkness*, and read slowly. It was a huge book, as thick as two fat paperbacks together, and she wondered yet again why it had not been published in two volumes, even three. Despite its size, she was savouring it, refusing to let herself rush through, and frequently looking up other books to check things.

Aria missed the iPad Mat had given her, "for Googling stuff". She had given it back, but he had returned it and she had allowed him to insist because, although she claimed to hate it, she probably searched for at least three things every evening. Now, as she read about Captain Fitzroy's foray at Valparaiso, she had to drop below briefly to find a map of Chile.

In the late afternoon, Aria did the 1700 hours recordings and peeled vegetables. 'Peel-em'n'boil-ems', her father called them. It was a mindless task that let her go over whatever needed a good thinking-out. She had hardly begun when the motor faltered and stopped.

Pssst!'s speed dropped away. She checked the gauges, which all seemed normal, restarted it, and all still looked okay. She dropped it into forward and it stalled. She restarted and tried reverse. It stalled. She cursed to herself.

She set the genoa and tweaked the sails to keep at least some way to minimize the roll and tapped on the cabin roof. Tap.

Taptap. Oscar's sleepy face appeared at the companionway. "Engine's broken down. Well, it runs but won't run in gear."

"I heard it stop and hoped you'd got some wind. I dunno what that would be—something come off, I suppose." He clambered into the crawl way and Aria heard bumping, muttering and cursing. "Everything looks alright," he yelled. He came up with his heavy eyebrows knotted. "I think it has to be the prop—something round it. Ted should have fitted one of those cutters I told him about."

"I should have insisted. That was the only way I got a barometer."

"Well, we could heave to again and I'll go over and free it if I can."

"No way! You should know that. You maybe haven't thrown anything over, but the least thing brings sharks. Look." She took her vegetables out of the mass of peelings in the bottom of the bowl, "See what happens?" The peels had hardly hit the water when there was a swirl and several small fins were momentarily visible. "You want that lot attached to your leg?"

Oscar gave his deep rumbling laugh and pointed. "Nor that one." Ahead of them, a large pale misshapen fin rose lazily and dropped away again. "I'm easily convinced. No clearing it, but what now?"

"We sail, wind or not. The wind's picking up, very slightly, from the east. I think it'll pick up more. Barometer's saying nothing, but I think that's a windy sky." *Pssst!* had gathered a knot or two and there was a chortle of water under her keel.

"Oscar, you put the vegetables on to cook and then come up again—it's lovely, really, without the motor."

The yacht glided gently with a dip to the swell, and they sat in silence, watching the empty horizon and the sun dropping towards it to port.

Oscar found butter in the refrigerator, and mashed it into the vegetables. He topped the mash with New Zealand canned mutton, his favourite. The mutton was salty and rich with fat and the buttery mashed vegetables tasted like baby food. Aria ate slowly and savoured it. "Mmm. Carlotta would be disapproving but well done—*delicious*."

Oscar grinned. "Crazy how food gets to be so important—brings more happiness than a motor that works."

***

Aria felt she had hardly been asleep when Oscar's voice reached her, urgency colouring his shout. "Whales to port! Come up quick, Aria. Whole pod, I think. They're close on the port side, but I can't see all of them."

"Oh, I've only … Come round to starboard a bit, if you think that will give us some distance."

Oscar stood open-mouthed behind the wheel. "Can't do anything. They're everywhere—we're in the middle of them, I think." The sea was lit only by pale starlight. Several whale backs showed darkly on their port side, moving more or less north-south. *Pssst!* gave a sudden lurch as one surfaced close by on their starboard side, making Aria lose her balance on the companionway. She kept her grip and scrambled to reach the cockpit.

A huge tail came down flat on the surface to port, sending a shower of water over them as Aria reached the deck. She could smell fish. *Pssst!* lurched. Oscar did not move, bare chested and grinning in the starlight, his muscles braced, wide eyes darting from side to side. "No contact—he just displaced a lot of water. Us with it."

Aria clung firmly to the sissy bar and peered over the sides. "I can't see any on the starboard side now, but there's quite a few to port. Hope there's none under us." She watched them sliding in and out of view in the dim light.

Oscar's voice was soft. "Stay calm. They're aware of us, of course—sussing us out, eh. Having a laugh, perhaps. They're humpbacks, travelling. I reckon they know more about us than you might think. Not only recognise a boat, but know there's people on it. The one that smacked its tail came up from underneath us, and didn't do it 'til he was well away. Just enough to give us a bath."

"Oh, really? Underneath!"

They watched the sea for more but the grey shapes and occasional flukes broke the silky surface further and further away, and were soon invisible.

"That's the show over. Hey, that was just fantastic, eh! Aren't they the most beautiful things?" Oscar's chiselled features were lit up with a wild grin. His laugh boomed into the night. He was dripping, careless and happy. "Your shirt is soaked, Captain. Better take it off."

Aria hesitated, imagining her hands on his wet chest. She turned away and dropped down the companionway.

Chapter Eighteen

In the forward head, Aria took a small plastic jug of water, stripped off her clothes and poured it over herself. The shower was a hose beside the toilet, the floor a shallow basin, but she would have needed to start the engine to activate the shower pump. She wondered if charter passengers were going to cope with this. They would probably be unaware that it is safer to shower sitting down on a yacht, so they'd simply find it primitive. But that was going to be Ted's concern, not hers. Perhaps Ted would motor from marina to marina, showers no problem.

Dry again, she peered into the small high mirror. She could see her one high, pointed breast and the messy scar, bright, puckered and uneven, across her left chest where infection had gnarled the skin. It was a long time since she had looked at it in a mirror. Her surgeon had promised a revision, but she dreaded more surgery, and her arm worked. It was, she thought, better to work with what she had. But could anyone look at that and not see it as horrible? Would she ever let anyone see her naked again? What would Oscar think if she dared to let him? At the thought of that, she felt a violent swirl of desire that almost drowned her fear. She clutched her arms across her chest and thought that she couldn't bear it if he was repulsed, if he rejected her—she would have to know him better; she would have to be able to trust him to care about more than looks. So no, not now.

Her bra was damp, but the padding on the left side dry so she put it back on, dressed in dry clothes and threw herself back in her bunk. She cupped her hand over her one still beautiful breast, pressed her face into the pillow and whispered, "Oh Oscar."

***

Oscar left her to sleep an extra half hour into her watch again. "Whale allowance."

Aria sighed. "It's twelve thirty. The watch times are *fixed*, Oscar."

"Yeah, I know, but I've had a great session—lots of dolphins and some schools of flying fish. I could have grabbed some in the scuppers, if you fancied a twisted corpse full of bones for a midnight snack."

"You didn't go out of the cockpit, did you? It's a firm rule, you know." She was holding one finger up, shaking it slightly. "I don't want to find you're gone. Forever."

"No, I didn't. I might have; it's a very easy sail. But I know— no going out of the cockpit alone."

"There's only you and me, remember. That rule is absolute."

A cheeky grin broke out. "Yep. You and me's good." He hesitated but she was scanning the horizon. "But Aria, it was a fantastic watch, with the whales and everything. That's what people call a humbling experience. I did nothing, and they were careful of *us*. I'm convinced they're rational creatures and don't randomly attack. But I reckon they deliberately sneaked up on me!" His face radiated happiness as he fussed around doing the 0100 hours log, sat chatting, made her a thermos of tea and himself a snack and was soon enough doing the 0200 hours readings as well.

"Go."

"I'm good."

"You're cluttering up my watch."

"That's not nice, eh."

But he jumped down the companionway, washed off the salt as Aria had and crossed to his bunk without a towel. His pe'a looked like board shorts in the faint light of the cabin lamp.

Aria felt a wave of sadness and turned determinedly to sailing. She brought the sheets in as the wind come round to the east and strengthened. *Pssst!* slid along again with the self steering working well.

The horizon was vague even though the stars were bright and clear above. Aria hoped the easterly would keep up all the way to Fiji, since that was the prevailing wind there. Towards daylight, she felt the wind was threatening and the seas much rougher. She knew it would be her imagination. The recordings showed little change; fourteen knots, easterly, with the seas building but, as yet, moderate.

***

As daylight broke, silver and gold blossomed through cloud. Aria read the log, tapped on the coaming and heard the squeaking of dolphins. Oscar appeared promptly, tousled hair falling over his shoulders. "Noisy beggers! Why can't they let a man sleep?"

"Because a man is now on watch. And he needs to reduce sail. We'll swap the genoa for the yankee. After breakfast will do. You're allowed a bit of fun." Aria moved to the galley and put on the strap. She did not really need it; *Pssst!* was heeled hard to port. She leaned into the corner, ready to grab a fiddle, and made porridge for breakfast. She ate it on deck with Oscar before he put up the yankee jib. It made little difference to their speed once it was set—*Pssst!* was sprinting—but it felt safer.

Aria chose the port settee and snuggled into the corner of it. Could life be any simpler or nicer, she wondered? But she did not fall asleep; she got up again and called Bree, though she did not tell her of the engine problem. She glanced at the chronometer and called Ted to remind him to send in their C2-C form, the photo of *Pssst!* showing its crazy name and a copy of her passport. Her voice was raised.

"Ted, you need to do it now. We are about two days away ... oh, today's Sunday? So send it *first thing* Monday morning—tomorrow. It's not really good enough; they are expecting not just a day but a *time*. But tell them we will probably arrive on Tuesday, latest Wednesday. It will have to do. We have no engine, so explain that we'll be sailing in ... yes, the engine doesn't work, so we're ... what? It stalls. Plastic or a line round the prop, I suppose. It runs but stalls ... no, the fuel's fine; the engine runs. I don't really know ,,. w*hat*? Ted, it's *insanity* to go over and clear it in mid-ocean ... he ... no, I *forbade* it. It's dangerous and not absolutely necessary ... Yes, sure, I am responsible as Captain. I accept that ... dammit, Ted, no engine is *no big deal*! I'll handle it. Goodbye." Aria brushed her damp hair roughly off her face and suddenly grinned. No big deal, she thought. We'll go through our first coral. It might be, yet.

***

When Aria came up with lunch, Oscar was playing the flute. *Pssst!* was bounding along with the self-steering working, heeled and throwing spray over the bows.

"Just a day or two more, Oscar."

The flute trailed off and Oscar peered north into the bright noonday light. "Fiji! I'm sure it'll be very different from Samoa. The Fijians are kind of half Polynesian, half Melanesian. Maybe that's what made the difference—having a coup and all that."

Aria handed him his lunch. "I think that was several things. Indians starting to outnumber Fijians, the burgeoning of nationalism everywhere in this overcrowded world, the UN sending Fijian peacekeeping forces to the Middle East." She grimaced. "I think violence and bullying are catching and those guys who went over there probably saw how to do it, made contacts amongst the arms dealers … the UN spreads the very diseases it purports to cure."

Oscar stared at her. "What sort of law do you do?"

"Not international law or human rights, but I take an interest. A lawyer always thinks, 'Who's behind this? Who stands to benefit?' The arms dealers in this case. That's usually the kernel: who gains the most. Those questions sometimes have surprising answers when you think things through."

***

Oscar brought his guitar up and played some Fijian and Samoan songs. Then he asked Aria what she'd like to sing, but each time she faded out. He carried on, singing song after song. "Haha! You know the first four lines of every song ever written, and *none* right through."

"I think I'm just distracted by your little trills and skirmishes. I'm sure I know all the words to *something*. Play something very plainly for me."

"Trills and skirmishes. Hahaaa! Here's a skirmish …" and he piled chords and notes on top of one another into a jangling crescendo, then stopped as a few drops of spray hit him. He put the guitar if its safe place below and came back to look up at the sails, hands behind his head. "Hey, you thinking of just single-handing enough to prove you can do it, or are you planning to do long passages—round the Pacific or round the world, even?"

"Either. Both, maybe. I'm like you—I just love being out here. But I have to wait and see what the future holds, so in the meantime, I'll do a single-handed passage or two. If I'm still around in five years—that's the sort of time frame I have to look at—I'll see."

The breeze was damp on their skins. Oscar rolled his head on his arms to look directly at her. His voice was low. "What do you mean *still around*?"

"I've had breast cancer; I thought you'd guessed when I said the operation wasn't on my shoulder. I was just twenty-nine when it was diagnosed, which is a bit grim. If I'm still well in five years, that's good news. Then I can think about ten."

Oscar was silent for a long time. "You're braver than I thought. So that's what your surgery last year was! Not for your shoulder, just affecting it. You're an amazing woman."

Aria smiled into the distance.

His voice was soft. "So what's the outlook for you?"

"Just that. Watch for five years and hope. Then watch and hope for longer. Bree's much more frightened about it than me, for both of us. It makes her very high risk—Mum and then me. Many people do survive it, you know. Twenty years, thirty years, I don't know, some of these women live to old age, I think." She shrugged. "But, what the hell, I just have to bear it in mind and do all these things I really want to do while I can." She looked at him sideways and grinned. "So yep, you've been sailing with an Amazon."

"Here's one for a remarkable woman." He retrieved his guitar and sat under the dodger to sing a sweet old Tongan song, *Ise Isa Viola Lose Hina,* his husky voice just audible over the guitar and the rustle of the waves.

***

On the morning of day nine, when they had not had a noon sight for two days, Oscar got up a little earlier and pored over the chart, then sat gazing forward. The wind was now over twenty knots. "Isn't this the day we should sight land?" He stood up. "All that cloud has to mean something. The rest is the usual lumps, but that bit's solid and it's where Fiji's supposed to be, if we're not lost."

Aria peered hard. "We're definitely *not* lost. Could be Fiji, I suppose, but I don't think we'll see it yet. Too far off. I dread having to negotiate the approaches and get into port under sail, somehow. Just hope we can do it. What'd happen if we hit a reef with Ted's boat?"

"Well, there's nothing like having to for making you succeed. We'll take it easy. It'll be fine."

"In this wind? It might be too much. But closer to the islands it might drop off a bit, I suppose … you know that *is* something up ahead."

Oscar stood tall and peered. "That's *land* under that thumping big raincloud—that'll be Fiji!"

Aria cooked up a huge breakfast of all the remaining bacon and eggs, heated a can of mushrooms and put them on toast. "Don't use up all the tucker." Oscar called down to her. "We might fetch up on a reef and eat raw shellfish like those five Tongans, until we're rescued months from now."

Her smile faded. "Don't joke. It's a possibility, of course; anything is, with no engine. Not five months, I hope." After breakfast, she studied the Fiji chart for an hour or more, working out bearings, distances, and identifying hazards. She only slept for a few hours.

The wind dropped to twelve knots and they both stayed up for the afternoon watch; their excitement was too great for Oscar to go below. Eventually, they identified Kadavu Island far on the starboard bow, watched it get closer and took turns to study the chart. The wind faltered and weakened and it was clear they had no chance of getting in to Suva in daylight. They put *Pssst!* about and sailed off west south west while still out in safe water.

Aria called Bree and left a message that they were almost there, but not going in until next day. "We'll sail away half the night and come back in the morning. I'll call you once we arrive."

When Aria called Ted to tell him, he was effusive. "Orya, that's great! My li'l babe is pretty fast, huh? Or is it her Captain? … Hey, it was just a joke." Then more seriously, "Listen, I've faxed it all, and scanned it and sent an email, a duplicate, to make sure. Well, great you got there safely—didn't need the engine, huh? You're some sailor-gal! You got news of Harky … no? Well, you're there tomorrow." When Aria asked if he was in Suva, Ted carried on, "Orya, I'll see you pretty soon. I'm just so pleased my li'l baby is safe and sound. Yella bye!"

"Oscar, what's this 'yella', Ted says?"

"It's a run-together of "Ya Allah", meaning, 'Oh God', and sometimes used as that, but it's a grab all to mean 'wow' 'let's go', 'come on', 'okay'—whatever, really."

"Ted avoided saying whether he's in Fiji or not yet. He doesn't make anything easy or straightforward if he can help it."

"He doesn't." Oscar laughed as he settled into his watch. "I'm in two minds, eh. Want to get there, and don't. I've never been so happy in all my life as these last four days with you. I'm cool with spending another night at sea, eh."

Aria felt the same but said nothing. She stayed up another hour, and they sat together in the dark, watching a couple of vessels. "Have to keep a pretty good eye on this course; we won't get another shot before we're going in to Suva harbour. It might be a problem if we get squalls." But she knew he would keep a keen lookout and mind his course carefully. "Oscar, wake me at three."

***

At 0030 hours, Oscar called Aria up and they went about. The wind was gusty and from the south-east again. Oscar went below and Aria spent the first half of her early morning watch keeping busy. She carefully did her log and noted the lights of an occasional vessel.

The last half, she spent nervously updating her position, monitoring various vessels, identifying as well as she could every pinprick of light. She was greatly relieved when Oscar came on deck again early, as the sky began to pale. "Oscar, I'm glad you're up. I'm nervous about this. I brought her closer to the western tip of Kadavu, 'cos it's safer. We're about twelve miles north of the peak behind Tavuki by my dead reckoning, so we'll get into the entrance … oh, a few hours, I'd say. That's the peak you can see. Our heading is 35 degrees at present. Check everything I've done, will you? Just in case? The breeze is messing about and I'm jittery being anywhere near these islands and Bega reef. I'll make us something to eat—nurture our brains and settle mine."

"If there's anything left after yesterday's feast. Hey, we'll sail in there like we've done it before. Be cool."

Aria laughed. "Mmm, except we haven't. When we get in, we need to go to a quarantine area over by the yacht club, north end of the harbour."

In daylight, the land grew larger. They were both jittery. They scanned the sea constantly, and Oscar jumped below several times to look at the chart. "Oscar, grab the Q and Fiji flags, would you? They're right there in the flag bag, top of the bosun's locker. Don't need them yet, but then they'll be ready. We're making good time; won't be long."

The wind changed direction by several points several times, as they passed the Bega reefs, well away. Aria watched Oscar fiddling about, never taking his eyes off breaking water. When the time came to make for the harbour, *Pssst!* was sailing sweetly. For a start, the morning light had been in their eyes, but when they headed north, Aria was able to negotiate the entrance with good visibility. As they burst into Suva harbour, she called, "Shorten sail and we'll make our way over there cautiously,

Oscar. Let our nerves settle. Oh, and run the flags up, would you?" She slowly eased off the yankee.

Oscar brought the main down to half its area very handily, and dropped the mizzen. It was the first time they had done anything much with it except set it, since Auckland. "Nearly forgot we had the old mizzen." *Pssst!* dropped her speed, straightened up and ghosted across the harbour towards the Yacht Club. They had not gone far when they were met and hailed by two Customs boats, which escorted them across the harbour, but following, not showing the way.

Two other yachts were waiting to clear in, Aria guessed by their yellow flags. "Is it here?" she yelled to a man on deck.

He had a white beard covering a weathered face that might have been at sea for years on end. "Just drop yer hook!"

She brought *Pssst!* round into the wind and Oscar sent the anchor rattling out. *Pssst!* drifted back and stopped, swinging slightly. "Done," she laughed as Oscar came back to the cockpit. He grabbed her in a hug that lifted her off her feet. "Done? *Well* done."

"Take it easy. That tells everyone you can't believe sailing in went alright. Who needs to be cool now?" He let her go.

The weather-beaten fellow called across, "Engine problem or just impressin' the rest of us?"

"Engine problem. We think we've fouled the prop."

"Jeez, well, don't go over on it here. This harbour's tight with sharks. Have her hauled out—there's a slip over there." He waved an arm. "Clean it up safely. That's my advice."

"Oh, okay. Thanks." And to Oscar, "Looks like Customs were waiting for us." The Customs boats pulled alongside, one to port and one to starboard.

Sailors on the other yachts with yellow flags flying watched. The Fijian officials, when they came alongside and boarded, were neatly uniformed and very formal. They already knew of the arrival of the HMNZS *Canterbury*, with its comatose passenger and Carlotta, and had been expecting *Pssst!* though they clearly disapproved of so few communications. "If you have a sat phone, you could have called the Harbour Master, RSYC, the yacht club, or Biosecurity. There's a penalty for failing to do this. You've had difficult circumstances, though …" No fine was mentioned again.

Clearly, Carlotta had made an impression; when her name came up, it was the only time that the formal atmosphere lightened, and one of them stifled a guffaw. Aria sat straight-faced, filling in forms.

"Where is the owner of the yacht? He must present himself here or to our offices straight away."

"The owner is aware of that, but I don't know if he's arrived from New Zealand yet. Certainly, if he contacts us, we'll let him know that you want to see him immediately."

"No need to tell him more than that he is expected at our offices, when he calls you." The most senior customs man and the biosecurity fellow exchanged quick glances and there was a hint of a nod to Bio. "Captain Stihl, there are certain, er … we are tightening up inspections here, at present. Your vessel will be subject to a thorough search. You might be required to take her out of the water as well."

"Yes. Please just let us know what you want. We need to pull her out anyway, because we think the propeller is fouled—that's why we sailed in."

"Then we will do that. You must remain on board for the inspection, above decks. Don't do anything."

"Could I rig an awning? It's under the cockpit seat."

He nodded, and stood at the companionway watching her lift the cushion and shake it out. He nodded again and she tied it between the mizzen boom and the stanchions. It would be inconveniently low, but offered shade and did not obstruct the cockpit.

Aria and Oscar sat under it on deck feeling sweat start to prickle. The air was steamy and still, and heat radiated through the canvas. The Customs men swarmed over the yacht, apparently working fast but even so, the search dragged. "They're going through every darned thing. More thorough than Manny, I'd say, and that'd be something." Oscar's laugh rumbled softly.

Below, the men began in the forepeak and moved aft. They ran their fingers into Carlotta's shoes which she had forgotten and painstakingly went through Harky's gear, even the smelly clothes. They removed every cushion, opened every locker, checked random books, every item in the galley, all the gear in the bosun's locker and navigation drawers. In Aria's cabin, they emptied her lockers onto her bunk. Aria thought of Manny's persistent interest in the boat and felt suddenly nervous. For the first time, she wondered if Manny had been looking for a good hiding spot and at Half Moon Bay had put something aboard. Her stomach lurched; she slowed her breathing and watched children playing in the garden of the yacht club.

Her mind raced back, looking for clues. But she had searched, too, long and hard, and found nothing. What was it about? She looked at Oscar.

He had stopped watching the search and was gazing out at the other yachts, alert and tense. He felt her eyes resting on him, glanced at her and pulled the corners of his mouth down. "Jeez, Aria."

"Mmm, I feel pretty sick, too. But you know, I inspected her very carefully at Half Moon Bay. After Manny came aboard. I'm now wondering … maybe he …" She grimaced. "These guys suspect something, I'm sure. The other boats were already waiting, and they came out to meet us. Now this. Not good, eh, but we can't do anything—just sit here."

Half an hour passed before the head Customs man came up, made a few phone calls in Fijian and told Aria that the yacht would be hauled out on the slip. One junior fellow would stay aboard.

The fees were paid and all left to the waiting yachts except for a solidly muscled young man with close-cropped hair and an inscrutably still face.

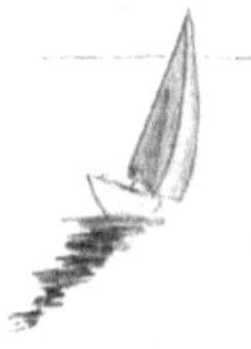

Chapter Nineteen

Hot and anxious, they dropped the awning and went below. They shared cool water with Sione, the remaining customs man, and waited for the immigration official to arrive on the club's rescue boat. The Immigration officers, too, were aware of the arrival of Carlotta and Harky, and very curious about the rescue procedure. They completed their paperwork quickly and efficiently, asked many questions about the *Canterbury* that Aria and Oscar could not answer and politely expressed hope for Harky's recovery. One of them began telling Aria the regulations for cruising in Fiji waters.

She interrupted him, "But we are just delivery crew. Our job is finished. We fly to Auckland as soon as the owner takes delivery of her and we get a seat on a plane."

"Then that, when other formalities are completed, should be very simple." Aria thought he must know their Customs inspection was not yet over. Eventually, he took the rescue boat to one of the other yellow-flagged yachts.

Aria called the Suva hospital. After much confusion and many transfers, Carlotta's loud excited voice came through. "You're here! Fantastic …"

"Lotta, how's everything?"

"Not too flash. But you've taken longer than I thought—been lookin' out for you … oh, really, then you've done okay. Nine, ten days is fine … No, Harky's not shown any sign of improvement. They say give him more time, but I don't think he's gonna make a recovery. It's … goddam awful. Hey, listen, I'll come down when they've done this scan … oh, Customs? You have to do that first? Now? Something wrong? Well, I'll hear about it soon!"

"And we need to hear about the *Canterbury* experience," but Carlotta had put the phone down.

At last, they received the go-ahead via Sione's radio to take *Pssst!* over to the yard. "This will be at Ted's expense, so I really ought to tell him we are doing it." Aria looked at Oscar.

He shrugged. "But where is he? Silly beggar. He wants the electronics put in so he'll have to pull her out twice—still, that gear might not be ready yet, or not here or anything."

"I just thought that'd all happen after we'd handed over." Aria frowned. "And where is he, to hand over to? That's the problem with making assumptions when you are dealing with boats—and Ted! Nothing works out as you expect."

Aria declined being towed over to the slip and they sailed over as slowly as they could. She was glad to have Sione aboard. She almost missed the cradle and yelled at Oscar when he used his foot to push her in, "No limbs off the boat!" The slip workers were shouting at everyone to stand clear as the wire ropes tensioned.

Oscar was about to argue that his foot was never in danger of being crushed but he thought better of it. Who'd risk being off-side with a skipper like Aria? He grinned at her. "I thought that yelling was limited to berthing and mooring and blocked heads and …"

She shook her head and laughed.

They were hauled up onto the slip, the creaking and groaning of the gear tearing at their nerves.

"They'll put a ladder up but don't move 'til we know we are chocked and safe. And even then, keep an eye on everything all the time. This has potential for accidents."

Oscar waited until they were stable and then he and Sione climbed down to join a few of the officials there to inspect the hull and keel. They tapped and poked and muttered.

Trailing far behind the propeller was a light polypropylene line with shreds of net, many barnacles and tangles of weed. At its other end, down the slip, were various pieces of degrading plastic. Oscar whistled. "You should come down and look at this. We had a sea anchor out. It's a wonder we aren't still out there."

The polyprop line had melted into a solid mass around the shaft. Oscar strained to cut it away with his diver's knife, his muscles bulging with the effort. Chunk by chunk, he hacked it off.

"You be ready to get out of there fast if anything looks like giving way," Aria called down to him. It all looked too simple to be a safe arrangement, and the thought of Oscar under the yacht while it was perched in the cradle and held in place by the wire ropes made her hair prickle. She stood motionless at the wheel.

It seemed too long to be reasonable before she heard him shout, "That's it."

Aria called down from on deck, "Oscar, just have a look for anything else. Check everything, especially the holes."

"No damage done, by the look, but it's not surprising the engine wasn't happy. I'll mention that cutter thing to Ted again." Oscar gathered up the long line of rubbish he had freed from the propeller and fed it carefully into a bin. He got a thumbs up from the Customs fellow, a ghost of a nod from Sione, and the customs people left. "OK! Finished. They've signed us off. All looks fine and inspection done. Back in the water."

"You go round on foot. I'll take her somewhere out there to anchor, and come ashore to arrange a berth. I don't care either way. But alongside might not be acceptable to Customs."

Releasing the yacht back down the slipway tore at their nerves even more. Oscar called up to her, "If only it didn't give those little jerks."

"We'll be in soon. Just need to make sure the motor and prop are working." Aria watched as the water enveloped *Pssst!* and felt her lift and right herself. Once she was free of the cradle, Aria started the motor, listened carefully, dropped it into reverse gear and when she was well away, turned and glided back to the anchorage. She brought *Pssst!* round head to the wind amongst others anchored off. A woman called out, "You're sweet there. Welcome. Come over some time."

Aria dropped the anchor. *Pssst!* sat gently back on it like a mildly reluctant donkey. She watched for a while, made tea and sat in the cockpit. She waited to be quite sure the anchor held, then launched the dinghy and rowed over to the club. "No outboard either?" called her erstwhile neighbour. She leaned back on the oars, pulling hard and it felt good after so much time aboard.

Oscar had gone round to the yacht club to look for Carlotta. The yacht club was a graceful old affair with an expansive view of the harbour, a generous bar and waiters in white. Shades of the colonial era hung about it, even though the drinkers were casual and noisy.

Carlotta arrived on a bus, jumped off before it was quite at a halt and screamed, "Fanny, am I glad to see you guys!" She hugged Aria and made such a fuss that the crowded bar through the doors fell quiet and heads turned. "Oh, I wish Harky was here with us, Aria. Come on, we need a good story-swap. I can't be too long. That navy ship—I gotta tell you—it was somethin' else! They can put on steam when they want to!"

Aria led her out into the garden. "Let me just talk to them about a berth on the pontoon. Don't tell Oscar *anything* til I get back. I want to hear every detail."

They sat and talked in the garden for a couple of hours, cold drinks tinkling with ice cubes and trickling with moisture.

Carlotta raised her beer glass. "To Oscar, the world's best crew. After me."

Oscar dropped his head, and laughed when Aria said, "Well, almost."

From time to time someone from the bar, eager for details of the mid-ocean rescue or getting onto the slip under sail, wandered across to join them. Some were keen for tips on how to deal with problems and some seemed keen to terrify themselves out of ever leaving port again.

Oscar got up. "Hey, all I can think of is meat and vegetables and fruit—I needed a day or two on the *Canterbury*. I'm off to the market. Wait for me? I'll ask inside where to go."

'Thanks, Oscar. Here—money from the ship's purse. Don't buy much. We're out of here as soon as Ted turns up, remember."

He was back a moment later. "There's a message from Ted at the office. He'll call *Pssst!* every hour. It's urgent, apparently."

"What? Where is he? What could be urgent? He should *urgently* come and take charge of his accursed boat. Damn him, I'd better get his call. When did he leave this message? Just now? Oh, it doesn't matter. Coming, Lotta? Oscar, I'll watch for you and pick you up."

Carlotta shook her head. "Nope—I'll go with Oscar and help get the stuff." Aria nodded and strode off to the dinghy. As Carlotta and Oscar walked out to the road together, Carlotta looked back at Aria. "That guy has no idea she dislikes him. He just doesn't get it. Haha!"

Back on board, Aria made tea and tidied ship while she waited. Ted was brusque. "Orya, listen. Makogai. Take my yacht over there right away and pick up Bree. She's …"

"No, Ted, I bloody can't! This yacht is not your limousine and I am not your driver. I would have to apply for a cruising permit to take the yacht out of Suva harbour. I could have done it when we cleared in but now my job is finished. You come and take over your boat and I'm going back to New Zealand as soon as you take her. I don't have forever and nor does Osc … hang on, *Bree's* on Makogai Island … here? What's Bree doing on Makogai?"

"Orya, just get the permit and I'll pay you extra. Do it, will you?" and he was gone.

She yelled into the phone, "*Ted*! *Wait*!" It was dead.

She punched the oars through the water as she rowed back to the yacht club with her papers. In the gardens, she walked up and down the paths until Oscar and Carlotta turned up, loaded with bags. By then she was calmer. "Just as well you did buy plenty. I'm now going to apply for a cruising permit. Bree's on Makogai and Ted says to take *Pssst!* and pick her up. What the heck is going on? Bree didn't mention coming to Fiji when I last spoke to her. She hasn't answered my last message. Maybe she came with Ted and didn't want to tell me 'cos she knows what I think of him. But Ted still didn't say if *he* is here. And why would she be on Makogai all of a sudden? It's insane." She shook her head, frowning.

Oscar was watching her, with a wide grin.

She glared at him and turned to Carlotta. "I don't know how long this permit thing takes, or when we're likely to get it. Lotta, do you need to get back to the hospital or could you help Oscar ready ship? I'll give you a whistle to pick me up. Hey Lotta, you want to come with us?"

"No, honey, I can't leave Harky for very long at all. They're nursing him fine, but I just have to be here for my own peace of mind. You two do it and I'll be around when you get back, if they don't airlift him or something. Oh, wow, Bree! It sure is intriguing!"

Aria leaped on a crowded open bus and rode into town. She walked down to the government offices. A tall Fijian in a white uniform sulu that managed to look nautical stepped up to her. "Yes?'

"I want to apply for a cruising permit, a sevusevu, for a yacht." She thought how attractive a man can look in a well-tailored sulu.

"Madam, you can do that at the marina. Did they not tell you?"

"No. But thank you. Is it quicker to do it here?"

"Well, yes, not much, but if you go to the sevusevu office ..." He described where to go. "And when you have it, you take it to customs for coastal clearance. Where are you going?" This last part was chat, she knew from his voice.

"Makogai."

"Just Makogai? You must call at Ovalau. I'm from there. And there are many more nice places further out—*so* many islands! Go to the Lau group if you have time. Don't just go to Makogai. It's a bit of a sad place, with many weeping ghosts."

"I'll see. Thank you, and yes, Levuka at least. That would be nice." She dashed off to the office, clutching her papers.

But the permit would not happen in one day. They told her they would send it to the Yacht Club when ready and she could pick it up from there. She hesitated, envisaging what would need to be done, and asked the officer if she could get the customs clearance there too.

"Yes, if the officers are there. They're there most days, with yachts coming in. We'll see if we can get your permit through soon, but don't be in a hurry."

She stepped out into bright sunlight. The perpetual Fiji cloud had a hole in it somewhere. "Well, only that my sister is waiting, that's all. But thank you, I'll collect it at the Yacht Club. That'll be good." The man was severely affected by vitiligo, only small patches of his original skin colour remaining and he put her in mind of her childhood horse Dallie, the ageing knabstrup she had learned to ride on. She felt a sudden surge of affection for all things dappled and vulnerable and imperfect.

***

When she got back, Oscar and Carlotta were waiting for her. "She's ready to go, Captain." Carlotta waved an arm towards the anchorage. "I even put a bundle of root aboard."

"Root?"

"That yaqona or whatever it is. You gotta have some of that as a present. I read up on Fijian etiquette. And don't wear your hat when you go to meet people."

"What? I can't go far without a hat."

"Fanny, just do what Mama Carlotta says, Princess. And don't stand when men are sitting. Sit too. You can't have your bits higher than their heads. When are you going? I assume that root's a long keeper."

"It's not instantaneous. I've applied and now all we can do is wait. I wish I knew what this is all about. I come up with a new theory every minute."

"Guessin' won't help, babe. Keep cool and make what haste you can. I'm sure it's all fine. This is just ol' Ted doin' his I-pull-the-strings and you-don't-ask-just-dance thing. He knows it drives you crazy. That's maybe why he does it. His way of flirtin'." Carlotta hugged Aria, gave her a local sim card for her mobile and told her to keep in touch. "Don't know if phones work there, but prob'ly not."

Aria and Oscar sat in the yacht club garden and ordered beer. Long afternoon shadows crept across the grass. Oscar stretched like a big sleepy cat. "Did you get a berth?"

"Yes, but now we don't want it 'til we return here. They're going to think I'm nuts."

"I'm sure yachties change their plans all the time. Make it up as they go."

"Apparently some do." She set her beer under her chair and jumped up. "Back in a moment."

Oscar watched her run across the lawn, weaving around chairs with an athletic grace. When she threw herself down beside him again, he raised his eyebrows in enquiry. She shrugged. "Yep, they were fine with that." She stretched. "I'll sleep tonight. Hard to imagine we haven't even been here a whole day yet. I feel in no hurry to get back to NZ."

He collapsed down again into a relaxed sprawl. "Yeah, this would do for a while." He sighed. "Ted's something, isn't he? Just as well we haven't got our NZ flights sorted out. I don't mind a little side trip, though. This is a beautiful place and a quick look at some of the islands when we get Bree aboard would be nice. Makogai is probably a good start. I'll look at the chart for the Lau group. And I could certainly do with some swimming and lazing about. Sometime, gotta think about what we'll do next, eh?"

"What next? Next delivery?" She screwed her head round to look at him. "You think we should do another?"

Oscar nodded. "Next sail of whatever sort. Don't know if I'd take another delivery. But I suppose each one's different, and we've learnt a bit. Don't you want to do more in the islands? We sail well together, eh. Should do more sailing together. You reckon Ted'd give you the job of charter skipper, now we know his tub so well?" He grinned and slid his eyes sideways to her.

"No. Absolutely not. I'm no charter skipper. I'd drown the chattering masses in their own champagne after one day. And I can't wait to get shot of Ted. You think I'd want to work for him again? I've got a perfectly good job—career—at home." She shook her head vigorously. "If I can't find decent people to work for, I won't take sailing jobs. I'll just do my single-handed passage in the Pacific Islands. And back."

"Yeah, but it's been great. Let's think about it. I just can't imagine getting home and getting all togged up and sitting in my office again trying to care what happens in the whatever department. Okay, not the charter boat thing, then."

Night was falling across the harbour, a soft thick darkness with a warm breeze that felt like a lover's breath on Aria's skin. "What made you go into that field if you're so bored by it?"

"Well, I'm strong in mathematics and when I started doing finance and economics, I never thought I'd be a glorified computer nerd like I am now, more or less. I wanted to get into international business specialising in Pacific Islands development, which is what I felt I ought to do to help all those families like my own. My Samoan family. Dad prays for them, but I think you have to do something more practical." He laughed up into the evening sky. "Then I started questioning that and changed over to philosophy. My parents had a fit. They both turned up in Christchurch—you should have seen it! The upshot was I dropped philosophy and completed the double degree. Not sorry about that, but just bored with this present stint."

"Philosophy. They were dead right. Most philosophy students philosophise themselves out of leaving their beds. And … well … philosophy's really just the sad history of men's bewilderment."

Oscar threw his head back and erupted in laughter. "You reckon? Men are bewildered?"

"Yep. *Born* bewildered. They have to be put on railway lines to achieve anything."

"And women?" His shoulders were still shaking and his eyes sparkled.

She shook her head, laughing. "Women are born knowing. That's why there are so few women who bother with philosophy."

His merriment increased. His head was screwed around to see her face straight on. "Well, you were, I reckon—born knowing. But … well, there are not many like you." His laughter bubbled up again.

"It's true with men. And the railway lines. That's what your parents did with you, in effect. When you derailed, they put you back on. That's what smart parents do."

He put his head on one side. "Dad's not bewildered, but that's because he's got God on his side. Mum … well, she probably doesn't think about it. Maybe as you say, she doesn't need to. She'll *do* something, won't analyse it or look for guidance first. Mmm, you might be right in Mum's case."

"I hardly know your parents. But your Dad definitely sounds like the leader."

"He is, in the community as well. It's his vocation, though. They're a good team, really."

Aria rested back in her chair, running drips off her glass with one finger. "I wish Bree could find that sort of person. One with a good heart who knows what he's doing is right. I think she'd be like your mother …just slot in and run with it very happily."

"Aw, you realise how often you say that? But there are very few of them around, I reckon. I'd *like* to be like Dad but I'm just not. I could never be that settled and reliable. And, besides, I go for decisive women, even if they're challenging." He slid a sideways glance at her, laughing again. "Might be a symptom of my bewilderment. Haha! Philosophy—the sad history of men's bewilderment!"

Chapter Twenty

It took another day for the permit to come through. During that time, Ted did not call or answer his phone and neither did Bree. But then Bree was on Makogai and who knew what telecommunications possibilities or impossibilities existed there? Aria even tried ringing Manny. "This is real desperation stuff, when I ring Manny," she told Oscar. But a robotic voice told her that Manny's phone had been switched off or disconnected. "It's like everyone's dropped off the planet. What do I do now?"

"Call the police. Say your sister and her friends don't answer their phones; say no one you know answers the phone. You'd like to report everyone you know missing. Better get a list ready." Oscar kept a straight face but for his eyes. "Look, you've got the permit, so get it to customs as soon as you can. Their launch is around somewhere this afternoon. I saw it puttering by just before you got back. That way, we could sail tomorrow."

"Yes, if we leave early-early and get a good breeze we'd be there late tomorrow. I don't quite dare do a night sail, but getting out of Suva very early on the lights would be ok. Then we'd do the sail in daylight and get there well before dark. We can't go in without good visibility."

"Hey, I do believe you're scared of coral."

"I certainly am. Only a nutter wouldn't be scared of the coral. I'm off. Back soon I hope."

She found the customs people sternly serving a notice to an unhappy fellow in the marina who looked gratefully at her for distracting them. Hers was a simple process, and they walked back to the offices with her. They were just finishing for the day, so she had been lucky.

Back on board, she had one more try at ringing Bree. No answer. "Let's eat and have an early night, then get up at three thirty and be under way by four o'clock, eh?"

Oscar nodded from the galley. "I've cooked stuffed chicken breasts with chilli tomato. And sweet potatoes. The green vegies are inside the chicken. And we can have the cold ones for breakfast."

"Well! You did claim to be able to cook. Of course I didn't believe you. Had a few too many cheese sandwiches. You might make a charter boat cook yet, if you can do something more than them. But leftovers for breakfast aren't big in chartering, you know. Umm … I'm setting the alarm for three thirty. You did check everything over with Carlotta the other day, didn't you? I'll do a run-around."

"Yep. Double checked everything. Ship shape and ready to sail."

"Let's eat on deck. It's a lovely evening." She carried some cutlery and paper napkins up, and took the plates from Oscar.

The sun was just setting, the heavy cloud glowing orange above it in folded layers. Around the town and anchorage, there were a couple of lights showing. Aria laughed. "It's rather early. But we'll be up three hours earlier tomorrow. This looks wonderful!"

"I had a look at the chart, and I see what you mean. There's a fair bit of coral. If all goes well, maybe we could spend a couple of days there with Bree. It'll be good for swimming and snorkeling. We haven't got wet on this whole voyage, except for the whales."

"Let's see. If Ted's with Bree, we might come back the same day." Aria pulled a face. "But yes, I think it looks like a good anchorage, so maybe. That might be nice."

They sat a little longer on deck after dinner, but a strong smell of fuel drifted across and drove them below. Aria held a handkerchief over her nose and breathed through several layers. Oscar said he quite liked it, but soon pulled his shirt up over his nose. "Whew! Makes me feel a bit zonked. Think we'll be okay?"

"Knocks out a few neurones, I believe. But we can hardly get away from it here. If we took to the dinghy, it would only be worse."

A breeze sprang up soon after and they again breathed the moist coconut sweetness of Fiji.

***

When the alarm rang, Aria found Oscar already up, making tea and singing in a strange little falsetto. He interrupted it to say "It's my Fijian good morning," then carried on. While his tea cooled, he pottered around on deck, still singing the high wistful song.

"Shh! The whole anchorage will think it's the Makogai ghosts crying in the night. The customs guy told me about them. He thinks Makogai is creepy." She was rewarded by a deep soft laugh and more singing. "We'll sail her off, if there's enough puff, eh? Try not to be a disturbance."

It was still dark when Oscar got ready to haul up the anchor, and Aria eased out the jib to give the yacht some way. The clatter of the anchor chain shattered the peace of the anchorage. Several people appeared on deck, so Aria started the engine, puttered noisily off, and crossed the harbour under a heavy sky.

In the gentle south-easterly, Oscar put up sail as soon as they were clear of the passage, and Aria cut the engine. There was nothing else moving. The lights were clear, though a strange bluish shade that they agreed might be difficult to see in rain.

They continued into easy seas on a beam reach until they were well out before bringing the yacht round, to clear the reefs along the coast. Then Oscar ran up more sail and *Pssst!* surged forward faster. By the time they were heading east for the south-eastern tip of Viti Levu, the sky was becoming light and a cool strengthening wind ruffled their hair. Aria stretched. "It's just so beautiful! Really, it would have been fun to sail as quietly out as we sailed in, but it was going to be too slow anyway. Breakfast's overdue as it is."

Gradually they passed the Nasilai Reef and came round more to the north east. It was a glorious morning and they dipped along on a broad beam reach with cold chicken leftovers, more tea and the sun in their eyes. "Captain, you *can't* say no to more of this island sailing. Come on, we gotta do it."

"Maybe. But different yacht, different deal."

"Different deal? You would sail with me again, wouldn't you?"

"Yes, you're alright." She went below to get a hat and sunglasses.

"Alright?"

"Stop fishing for more. You won't get it." But she got that laugh.

They had to tack several times. When the wind swung round to the north east, there was a delicious smell of coconut and smoke. The north-east wind did not last long; within half an hour it veered back to a south-easterly. Oscar said it was going to play games with them but he clearly enjoyed the tacking. Before noon, they were off Levuka and Aria thought of the fellow at the port offices and of the pictures she had seen of the old-fashioned main street of Levuka. Perhaps, she thought, life could be too simple; that's why he has a job in Suva instead. But simple was appealing.

By early afternoon, there was a dark bank of cloud building up. They had passed Ovalau and were confident of their position and course, but Aria began to feel anxious about visibility if there were squalls. The wind continued to play tricks until it was strong and astern so that they were running downwind, *Pssst!* bouncing along like a galloping horse. Aria kept a good eye on the build-up and saw that the cloud was gradually lowering and a squall developing. When the wind swung again to a southerly, directly into it, she knew it would hit them before long. The sea was now a gun metal grey with big white caps. Aria kept searching for the smash of waves on coral, but it was always well off and she was careful of her course. She wanted to be into the bay at Makogai while they had good light, not picking their way through the reefs in strong winds. "Wind's dropping off a bit, Oscar, and shifting a bit. There's quite a big squall building up."

Oscar reefed the main and mizzen down to half and partly furled the jib. "Think that will do for a bit? Slowed her up. I need to go below. Gotta." He looked at the darkening cloud and swung down the companionway.

Aria grimaced and nodded. "Well, be quick. Won't be long before it's on us. We'll need to shorten sail again, or maybe drop some."

Oscar was singing happily in the head, when she called down to him that they needed to drop some sail. The black tower in the sky was looming closer and the light had turned a peculiar yellowish grey.

She heard him shout that he was coming, and yelled back, "Come on! It's a heavy squall and closing faster than I thought!" The wind dropped to almost nothing and Aria hastily furled more of the jib. The reefed main gave a flap or two before she caught the wind in it.

Oscar emerged and clipped the door behind him. He had nearly reached the companionway when a sudden hard gust struck. It hit with such a wallop that *Pssst!* was knocked down. She rolled hard onto her port side.

Aria was thrown against the side of the cockpit but flung an arm around the mizzen mast to steady herself and held tightly to the wheel with one hand. She regained her balance as *Pssst!* righted herself, flipped off the jib sheet and stopped it again, yelling, "Oscar! Oscar, you alright?"

Below, Oscar had lost his footing and grabbed the fiddle of the bosun's locker with both hands. Books and other gear flew off the starboard shelves in the saloon. The clutter on the navigation table cascaded amidships, pouring noisily over the fiddle. He was thrown up off his feet, and found himself hanging by his arms. The whole bench in front of the doors lifted up on two arcs of steel at either end. When *Pssst!* righted herself and his feet found the floor, he was looking below the elevated bench of the bosun's locker at the jumbled contents of the two drawers. Between them, a narrow locker was filled with neatly secured plastic bags of something white. He paused half a moment, open-mouthed with astonishment, then bolted up the companionway.

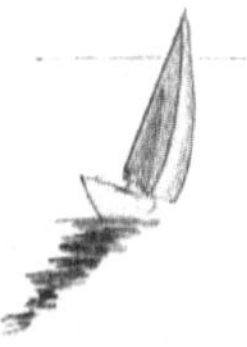

Chapter Twenty-one

The yacht was tearing along, lee rail awash and the sails straining. "Oscar, get the main down! We'll get hit again for sure!" Aria was balanced with one foot jammed hard against the seat back. Oscar did it like an automaton, negotiating the sloping wet deck and working fast. *Pssst!* settled down. She still rushed through the water at top speed but now felt better controlled. Several more powerful gusts gave her a good roll. Oscar held hard until she righted, before he regained the cockpit and sat down heavily. He wiped sweat across his forehead and swore.

Aria kept her eyes on the sails. "What's the matter? It's okay. You were just too slow. No damage done; the rigging didn't hit the water."

"Aria, give me the wheel. Yeah, I can handle it. You need to see below. *Don't touch anything*!" He got up and took her place, breathing through his mouth. "Go on—go below."

Aria looked at him curiously; she had never seen his face like this. She dropped down the companionway as the rain started slashing down. "I'll get the oilies out … oh … what's happened … oh Oscar! We're carrying drugs!" She appeared at the hatch. "What is it, Oscar? The white powder? How come we never found that space? It *is* some sort of drug, isn't it."

"I don't know. I think white powder can be lots of things. Don't touch it, that's all. And don't worry about the oily—I'm soaked. I need to cool off."

"This is … if it's drugs … it will be … we're in an awful mess. What'll we do?"

"I don't know. It's a lot. The hull slopes in but that locker is about eight centimetres wide and a metre deep. That's a lot of stuff. Just leave it, Aria. Come up here and sit under the dodger for a moment. Collect your wits."

Aria scrambled up the companionway as if she could not get away fast enough. The rain stopped as suddenly as it started. The wind had steadied and come round to the east-south-east. She took the wheel. "All I can think is that Bree is mixed up with this. I s'pose she must be. Oh God, Oscar, it's unbearable. I can't … I'm in a cleft stick."

"Just be calm. Sit down and think what we ought to do. Give me a minute." He shook out the reefs in the main and mizzen, then checked his course and adjusted the headsail. They were now on what he called a 'sweet tight reach' though the wind was still too strong to be called sweet. Oscar shivered; water dribbled out of his hair, down his body and dripping wet shorts. "Aria, listen, we have to go back to Suva and hand it over— hand the boat over. It's all we can do …" There was silence apart from the rush of water and wind and the creak of the rigging. "Aria?"

She was sitting with a blank face, eyes filled with tears. After a while she took a deep breath. "But Bree? I … I have to think, Oscar. You and I … God, I don't know what will happen to us, but at least we had nothing to do with it deliberately. But Bree …" The tears broke and poured down her face.

"You're b..."

She rounded on him. "Oh, for pity's sake. Leave me alone! This is a disaster and you're taking advantage of it. Stop it."

His big face fell, he blinked, his mouth opened and no sound came out. He was going to say, "You're best to turn back now."

She threw her palms up for a moment and let them drop. "Oscar, this is serious." Her voice was shaky. "Really serious. It's not *just* Bree. We might go to jail and then it's your job as a trusted bank officer, your parents' position in their community, my professional standing. There could be no end to the damage." The corners of her mouth turned down. "But for Bree it might be infinitely worse. Bree might get a mega jail sentence, depending on her part in it." She curled into the corner of the seat and for a few minutes sobbed uninhibitedly.

The wind was easing a little and now holding steady from the southeast. Oscar scanned the seas constantly, remaining aware of the dangers.

"Aria, I know all that. But we can only get through it by doing the right thing. We have to go back to Suva and hand *Pssst!* over. There's no alternative, Aria. We can't do anything else. We can't just get rid of it and cover up …dump it overboard or something. It's not right." He glanced at her; was she even listening? "Aria …?"

"No, Oscar. I mean, yes. I know we have to hand it over in Suva, but … I need time, for God's sake. If we reach the entrance soon, sail past and then we'll come back when I've had time to think." She stood up and turned, wet-faced, to the wind.

Oscar looked at her with the wind dragging her hair back. Her strong, perfect profile was marred by a stream of tears pushed horizontally by the wind. He saw the beacons marking the entrance but sailed past them. On they rushed for the markers to the northeast. He had not studied the chart except as far as Makogai. He leaned forward. "Aria, listen. We need to do a nav update. We need to know exactly where we are and where we're going."

She did not acknowledge having heard him.

"*Aria*! *Navigate*! We're in coral. We've got to know where we are!"

She moved absent-mindedly to the wheel. Not knowing the extent of Bree's involvement was frightening. Could they just go back to Suva? Leave Bree to do whatever she might once she knew what had happened? Aria felt a physical pain in her chest. Bree's life looked like one of privilege though it had felt, Aria knew, like one of loss. Society might judge her very harshly. "Oh Bree," she whispered, "I'm so frightened for you."

Oscar took bearings, dropped down the companionway, and pulled the chart out of the chaos on the cabin floor. He found the things he needed, leaving the rest. "Not easy in this jumble," he called up to her.

"Just do your best." And then, as the sun burst through rips in the cloud and glinted off the still rough chop, she thought, Bree would not knowingly do this. She might be dreadfully gullible, but she is not dishonest. She saw the way forward with instantaneous clarity. Whatever the consequences, she said to herself, Bree must take responsibility for whatever involvement she has had. I'd be wrong to compromise my belief in the law and due process. I will help Bree all I can, but I cannot shield her, and she might not need it.

Oscar popped his head out, but before he could speak, he saw that something had changed. Aria stood very straight, head high, peering forward. The tears had crusted at the corners of her eyes and left salty streaks across her face. Even so, she looked Amazonian to him.

"Oscar, let's put her about for Makogai. Have we got sea room? We will pick up Bree as planned and go to Suva. You are right. I'll help Bree all I can but she'll have to bear the consequences of any part in it. If she's with us when we go to the police—if she's part of the disclosure thing—it will help her case. I'll advise her to do that. She has to make up her own mind what she does, of course."

Oscar looked at Aria's set face and tight jaw and realised that indeed the decision was made. *Pssst!* was now sailing sedately but fast, all effects of the squall gone. Oscar scanned ahead. "OK, if that's your decision. I've done a quick nav update. We're safe; just do a reciprocal course, essentially. Wind's good for that. We go on to Makogai, get Bree, and go back to Suva. It'll be a night sail, of course."

"We'll do a night sail. We can. I wish I knew Bree's part in this. And it would help to know where Ted is."

"They'll find him. That's the least of our worries. We need to make sure we do the right thing." Oscar took a deep breath and said no more while he went about the log recordings. He, too, was afraid for Bree, but he knew he would not compromise either.

Aria held the wheel with her shoulders back and head high, damp hair flying.

***

They came back down past Makodroga Island, turned to port around the western point, and gave a wide berth to the fringe reef on the southern tip. Outside, the wind had been fair but the seas vigorous. It was now mid-afternoon. The sheltered water within the bay was calmer as Oscar jumped down the companionway and made a quick pot of tea. Further in, Aria looked across a pretty anchorage.

"We can sail in and drop our anchor well out. Need to stay away from the other yachts." She raised her eyebrows and he nodded. "Oscar, I think you had better try to close that damned thing. Put your hands where you think you had them before and see if it slides back shut. Someone from the island might have to come aboard. I don't know how things go here." She drained her tea cup.

He tried, at first gently and then with more and more force and then with jiggling and thumping but it would not close. "Maybe I bent the runners. I wrenched it up and had my full weight swinging on it when I fell backwards. We'll have to leave it and hope no officials come out. Don't know if they have anyone here or not. We should've read that up." He had earlier scooped up some of the navigation gear, just gathering what he needed to plot their position and work out how to enter the anchorage. The books and everything else from the starboard shelves had skimmed the saloon table and fallen on the floor and port settee.

"Yes, I wish we had. Well, I think as soon as we've anchored, I'll go ashore in the dinghy, see if there's an official I should report to and find Bree. I wish bloody Ted had said where she's staying. But there can't be many places. On the chart it looks like there's really only one settlement and the school in the south. I think we should get Bree aboard and leave as soon as we're able. We need to be out of the reefs before dark, if we can. If I find her soon, we could do it. We could be in Suva early tomorrow." She pulled her mouth down in an exaggerated grimace. "Then let all hell break loose however it does."

They sailed in toward the scatter of vessels in front of the little settlement, turned to windward, luffed and felt *Pssst!* slow. When Oscar dropped the anchor, *Pssst!* came up short and drifted back while he let chain run out. "Sweet!"

They seemed to have good holding and were well away from the other yachts but still not very far from shore. Oscar took some bearings and jotted them down, then set about putting the dinghy overboard. They lay gently to the wind. "Off you go. I'll watch the anchor—no squalls, I hope—and keep an eye on the deck. If anyone comes, I'll make sure they don't go below. Ah, haha! I know! I'll tell them not to come aboard because the sewage holding tank has overflowed."

Aria flicked him a brief smile, tucked her sevusevu and crew list into her bra and climbed into the dinghy. "It has, metaphorically."

Oscar watched her row towards shore, avoiding the other boats. He folded his arms and rocked, as he did when thinking something out. The sun glinted on a now gloriously clear blue-green sea which reminded him of Samoa. He thought of his parents. "When you're in a mess, son," his father had said when he was a little boy, "Don't think about how to wriggle yourself out of it, think 'what is the right thing to do?'. Then it will work out well in the end." It had always been good advice. Oscar checked his bearings. It was a peaceful scene. There were only four other yachts. He crossed his legs and propped his chin on his fist. The right thing to do was definitely to go back to Suva and hand over the boat and its cargo. Time did not really matter, but they needed to do the reporting themselves.

He looked round at the entrance to the bay. On one side there was a small stretch of white beach with a little island joined to Makogai by rocks and coral. Small breakers curled over reefs fringing the bay. On the other side, further out, a small patch of sand was visible on the southern side of Makodroga Island.

A fishing boat, still far out, was coming in, perhaps from the reefs. Oscar remembered that the fishing areas are called iQoliqoli in Fijian and smiled at the word.

In the other direction, he saw that Aria was at the beach. His mind came back to their situation. Aria was not doing the wrong thing but it worried him to involve Bree at all. He wondered if he should have convinced Aria to return to Suva immediately, leaving Bree here and letting that, whatever it was, take its course. He frowned. No, perhaps Ted was here with her. Perhaps Ted had her where he could use her as a lever—a hostage even—if things went wrong for him. And they *had* gone wrong. What might Ted be capable of, if he was in the drug trade? People became pretty ruthless to survive in it. Would he kidnap? Would he kill? Oscar mused on what extremes Ted might go to, if cornered. He realised he was letting his worries run away and imagined his mates saying, "Aw, come on, bro!" He and Aria would just have to wait and see, he thought, take things as they came and do what's right as best they could.

He stretched and looked back across the anchorage, where he could see Aria on the beach with someone. They sat down. He had a sudden feeling that everything would work out right. If Aria was lucky and found Bree soon, he thought, he had better clean up below decks and have the yacht ready to go. He couldn't touch anything to do with the bosun's locker, but he could tidy up the litter of navigation gear on the galley floor. That was the most needed stuff. The rest on the cabin floor, between the settees and under the saloon table, he might just leave, depending on time.

Oscar went below and picked up the rest of the navigation instruments, pencils and a few plastic boxes that had jumped the high fiddle behind the stove as the yacht righted herself. Fortunately, no lids had popped off. Then he started on the saloon floor.

There was a bump against *Pssst!*'s hull, and a roll as someone boarded. He caught his breath and cursed himself for not keeping a better watch. He could see only a folded up trouser leg out the porthole. It could not be Aria and Bree. A glance out the opposite porthole showed Aria sitting on the beach where she had met the Fijian. He got up from the saloon floor and moved to keep whoever it was on deck.

Chapter Twenty-two

Aria rowed ashore past the scatter of boats. No one hailed her and there were no dinghies attached, so she assumed everyone had left their boats and gone to the island. She would be reluctant to do that, even in so sheltered a place, after the squall they had just faced. She enjoyed the hard work of the oars, but her mind raced ahead to what she should do to find Bree. Avoiding the area where old iron hospital beds from the leper colony were being used to promote marine growth, she came in near the jetty and stepped ashore on the beach. She pulled the dinghy up minimally; it was too heavy for her to shift much, so she toppled a large stone onto the painter. She retrieved her sevusevu and crew list from her shirt.

When she turned, an elderly Fijian man was walking down towards her. He was tall and wore a shirt and lavalava rather than the formally tailored sulu that she had seen in Suva. She walked towards him, wondering if he was the head man; she had no way of telling. Close to her, he nodded and put his hand out.

Aria held out her sevusevu and amended crew list and he accepted them solemnly. He took his time to check them, nodded again and handed the sevusevu back. She offered the newspaper-wrapped bundle. He did not take it but the ghost of a smile flicked across his eyes. He indicated a patch of shade and she sat down.

It had been, so far, a wordless exchange. She did not know if he spoke English or not. "I've come to meet my sister who's staying on Makogai, but I don't know where. Are there some places to stay?"

The man had squatted beside her, slightly higher up, which meant she had to turn to see his face. She passed the bundle of yaqona root across to him and he placed it absently beside him. He pressed his lips and gave a vague shake of his head. It could have been a no. He was gazing out over the anchorage with a calm, almost sleepy look.

"A young woman with blonde hair? She might be with someone else, I'm not sure."

Again, Aria received only the slightest response, only the slightest hint of a negative answer. The old man was watching a fishing boat coming in from sea. "Levuka," he said, but she had no idea of whether he was telling her the fishing boat came from Levuka or Bree might be in Levuka, or that people stay in Levuka and come by boat to the island. It could have meant anything.

On *Pssst!*, she saw that Oscar had gone below, and when she thought of the situation on board, was grateful for this enigmatic exchange. She would not want anyone coming out to the yacht for her sevusevu. She tried again. "Where would I look for my sister? Do people stay here? Is there a hotel or guest house where she might be?"

Behind her two couples were walking towards the jetty. One woman was tattooed so chaotically and extensively that Aria thought she must surely be Australian.

Again, her companion gave little acknowledgement that she had spoken, only a slight jutting of his lower lip and a lift of his hand.

She assumed the answer was negative. But if there was nowhere to stay on the island, where had Bree been for the last few days? What if she did not find her? She felt hot tears prickle behind her eyes. Why did Ted say she was here when it seemed very likely that she was not? She wished she had found out more about Makogai before they had set off.

She waited, wondering if the man did not speak English or if he was simply taciturn. She gazed out with him, the man sitting companionably enough beside her, after a while poking a hole in the package and examining a bit of yaqona root. The two couples were readying their dinghies near the jetty, chattering together noisily. She wondered if she could ask them if they knew of people staying on the island.

Then Aria noticed that the fishing boat was still behind *Pssst!* and someone had climbed aboard. Could it be Bree? She felt a surge of hope. But no, it was too big a person to be Bree. Who could it be? Where was Oscar? To her horror, he did not come up and whoever it was stepped into the cockpit and bent to go below. Alarm flooded over her. She would have to go back to *Pssst!*, see who was aboard, and decide what to do. She jumped up. The man stood too, watching.

Oscar appeared on deck, went forward with whoever it was behind him and hauled up the anchor. Why would he shift the yacht? Was he going to move *Pssst!* closer? *Pssst!* drifted backwards until Oscar trotted to the cockpit, bent to put the engine in gear and took the wheel. The other person followed him closely, then went below. Why did Oscar allow that, she wondered. Who was it?

Aria thought Oscar must be coming in closer to signal her to come, and she turned to the Fijian and smiled, getting a nod in return. He stood up, pointing at *Pssst!*. The yacht was moving forward under motor. "Thank you, I'll … Oh …" She ran. She saw Oscar slowly turn the yacht towards the sea. She shouted *"Pist!"* because that was the only way she could yell it,

"*Piiiiiist*!! *PIIIST!!*" but she knew she could not possibly be heard.

She ran toward the two couples, calling "Please help me—oh my God—my boat's going. I have to get out to it. Can you tow me please? Quickly?" She looked out at the boats again. *Pssst!* was chugging slowly and steadily out in the wake of the fishing boat far ahead. She ran to her dinghy, freed the painter and pushed it out with more strength than she thought she had.

One couple started their big motor. A short thickset man, weighing the stern down heavily, called, "That's your boat? Leaving? Jump in with us. We might catch 'em. What's happened, do ya' reckon?"

"I don't know. Someone went aboard her and now they're leaving." It occurred to her it *must* have been Bree, but why would they leave without her? Oh, but who knew what Bree was doing? "Can you tow me? I can't leave our dinghy behind."

He swirled his dinghy round close to her. "Gimme your painter. It'll be slower. But we mightn't have much hope of catching up anyway. You're prob'ly too late. Might see us, but." He took her painter and towed her, holding the painter wrapped around one hand and his foot on the knot, his other hand steering.

"Thanks!" she yelled over the noise. He was motoring hard, Aria's dinghy weaving in his wake. She put an oar over the stern to steady it and they increased speed a bit. They were past the anchored yachts but *Pssst!* was almost out of the bay, abreast the rocks on the nearest tip of Makodroga Island. What was Oscar doing? Should they even try to get out there, in a dinghy?

The guy in the dinghy pushed at the throttle but his outboard was already going as fast as it could go. She hoped he could handle it skilfully. Aria was getting a rough ride. They roared on as she held hard to steady her dinghy, hoping it would not capsize.

"Strewth, will you look at that? He's gonna hit that reef! What …?"

Aria saw Oscar had turned sharply to starboard and sped up. She saw *Pssst!* strike the reef, rear up with a huge chunk smashed off her keel and a gash in front of it and be dropped. The yacht surged forward on the next wave, tripped and heeled over. The hairs on Aria's arms were standing up and she tingled all over. The couple in the dinghy yelled, "Jeez, ya see that? She's gone!"

Aria's dinghy took a big splosh and she bailed it quickly, holding hard to her steering oar. When she looked again, *Pssst!* lay careened and almost still but for the occasional lift of her stern on a wave. When they got close, they could see that the gash in her hull and the splintered keel were out of the water. There was no one in sight. Where was Oscar? She screamed, "Oscar! Oscar!"

***

The fishing boat was not too careful of his topsides, but he supposed they would not understand a rebuke so said nothing. He had given them the second half of their fee as they approached and they were clearly pleased. As the boat bumped into the side of *Pssst!*, Ted snatched at the gunwales and the base of a stanchion and swung himself up. There was no one on deck but an empty tea cup had been left on the cockpit seat. He stepped into the cockpit and moved nimbly to the hatch. Leaning in, he called, "Orya? Oscar? Howdy!" He blinked and opened his eyes wide but the sunlight outside had been very bright and the cabin seemed black.

Oscar stood speechless for a moment, wishing he had not been so preoccupied. "Agh … Ted!" He had no idea of what he was going to do or where this was going.

Ted took a few steps down gripping the rim of the hatch firmly and bending forward into the cabin as his eyes became accustomed to the dim interior. "You guys took your time getting here. Good time in Suva, huh? Coupla three days …" He saw the open compartment, the bosun's bench raised above it. "What the hell? … Oscar! What the hell is going on here?" He lifted a foot from the companionway and pushed Oscar's shoulder hard making him stumble back against the edge of the table.

Ted came on down, his fists balled as soon as he no longer needed them. "You goddamn …" His voice was furious. "What are you up to here? Where's Orya?" He stumbled forward, grabbed the bench and tried to force it closed. It did not budge. "Oscar, close this goddamn thing. We gotta get outta here. Close it, will ya?"

Oscar was standing holding the pillar with one hand, the other outstretched, palm up towards Ted. "We're not going anywhere just now, Ted. You go where you like. We are taking this lot to Suva." He was surprised by his calm, firm voice; it was disembodied, a ventriloquist speaking. He hoped Ted took him seriously. His voice might not waver but his mind felt remarkably blank.

"Like hell you are! Start the engine, Oscar, get the anchor up. We are leaving right now, and while we go, I'll think where. The Laus, maybe—yeah, we'll go to the Laus. Or maybe a more distant group. The Solomons…."

Oscar stared at him, wondering if he was crazy, wondering if he could delay long enough for Aria to get back, wondering if Ted was perhaps sane and serious.

"Where's Orya? Huh?"

Oscar did not answer.

Ted's voice was low and threatening. "Oscar. Start the engine. Go lift the anchor. Don't make any move."

Oscar looked down at Ted's hand and saw he was pointing a gun at him. Where did it come from? It was a damned heavy-duty looking thing, and Oscar's mouth went dry. He heard himself say, "That won't make things any better for you, Ted. Put it down. I'll do it." But I am certainly *not* sailing him and this mess to the Laus or anywhere else, he thought. I'll have to do something.

Ted knew they were too far away for anyone to see the revolver. He kept it close to his ribs, aimed at Oscar's chest, and followed him up to the bows. Oscar worked mechanically, delaying as much as he dared. With the anchor up, *Pssst!* drifted backwards, but no one, if there were any other yachties on the other boats, noticed.

The fishing boat had gone in a wide arc and was now chugging quietly out of the bay. Oscar moved back to the wheel, very aware of Ted, close and threatening, started the engine, dropped it into gear and moved off. He made a slow, wide sweep as he brought *Pssst!* round towards the broad opening of the bay. Aria must have seen them. Oscar glimpsed several people running on the rough beach and thought one of them was Aria. He wondered whether she had found out anything of Bree and what she was thinking as she saw them readying to head out to sea. He felt sorry for her. What would she do? He did not look again, in case it drew Ted's attention to her. Another yacht was sailing in and he watched it. "I've got to slow down for this yacht. It's under sail."

Ted saw that they were going to pass close to the yacht coming in and went backwards down the companionway.

"Oscar, just get going. I'll have this gun on you every second, don't you forget that, so don't do anything smart." Ted stood in the cabin, leaning forward against the steps, the gun trained on Oscar where it could not be seen even if the yachts passed close to one another. "Don't you make a move, man. Don't you try anything."

Oscar stared ahead, puttering as slowly as he could out of the bay. There were rocks at the southern tip of Makodoga, and then a little strip of sand. His mouth was dry and he could feel his heart thumping at his ribs. He did not acknowledge the incoming yacht's wave and when they were past, gently turned the wheel more and more to starboard to bring them in close to Makodoga.

There was a tiny patch of beach on Makodoga and he tried to remember the chart. Was there a stretch of reef before it or just the little beach? He had not really looked at Makodoga. Ted was watching him. Oscar kept his face impassive and his gaze high as though he was looking out at the ocean and reefs ahead. The waves built as they left the bay.

Now! He turned the yacht towards the beach and sped up the motor, steering straight for the sand, keeping his eyes still

Ted was confused by the change in speed. "We outta the bay already, Oscar?" he yelled. He ducked his head to look out one porthole and then another, alarm showing on his face.

Without a clear thought, Oscar left the wheel, bounded like a big cat to the hatch and jumped down on Ted. He gave a terrifying yell as he launched himself down the companionway.

He knocked Ted down and pinned his gun hand to the floor with one arm. Ted was grunting and struggling. Oscar pounded a violent punch into Ted's jaw and heard his teeth come together with a whack. Ted's head rolled back. The revolver fired one bullet through the cabin roof above the galley. Oscar's knuckles hurt but he grabbed the gun and flung it behind him. It clattered down below the gimballed stove. It did not matter where the gun was now; Ted was out cold.

As Oscar got up, *Pssst!* struck a reef with a loud crack and a dizzying upward lurch. She hesitated before a wave lifted her further and dropped her hard with a splintering sound. Water spurted briefly from somewhere. Another wave caught her and she rushed forward, stumbled, and fell to port on the beach.

Anything still on the shelves cascaded off and Oscar fell on top of Ted. Ted was lying still and Oscar thought he might have overdone the punch. He felt faintly sick. He checked for a pulse and watched Ted's chest rise and fall for a moment. The bows must be out of the water, he thought, because the cabin sole was wet but not flooded. A small amount of water trickled in the bullet hole. The engine was running on high revs and each time the propeller was submerged it bit into the water and pushed, little by little forcing *Pssst!* round at an angle and further onto the beach.

Oscar struggled to stand with the yacht lying at such an extreme angle; the cabin floor was a steep wet incline. He got his feet against the lockers, grabbed Ted under the arms and heaved him straighter up the slope. Ted's head would stay out of water, if it did not come in faster, until help came. He assumed someone would have seen them. He lifted one of Ted's eyelids and looked with alarm at his rolled-back eye. He hoped help came soon.

Oscar scrambled up the side of the companionway, his feet slipping on the varnish, suddenly amused at the weird orientation of everything, the extreme incline. He laughed aloud. That's shock, he thought, I have to keep my wits clear and stop the engine, and see where we are and make sure Ted stays alive. He steadied himself, holding the side of the hatch.

Coming out of the bay, a dinghy towing another was streaming towards them, its bows pushed high above the water, spray flying. Some more dinghies and an outrigger canoe followed with outboards roaring. The incoming yacht had dropped her sails, turned and was coming back under motor.

Oscar stopped the engine and saw that *Pssst!* was not lying in much water at all. He had the sudden thought that she was going to be darned hard to get off, that far onto the sand with a reef behind her, and he started to laugh. Great gusts of laughter shook his ribs. He had no idea what he should do. He sat in the angle of the cockpit, to port, his feet almost higher than his head, where he could see if Ted moved or the cabin started to flood. He was rocking with laughter and knew he needed to stop.

The fellow in the lead dinghy tipped her outboard up and glided over the reef, then dropped the painter of the one he was towing. Aria! She stood and used her lone oar to get to the beach. The newly arrived yacht had slowed her motor and was dropping her anchor still some way out and a woman was filming on deck.

Oscar got up, still shaking with laughter, and saw Aria jump out of her dinghy and his laughter caught hard in his throat. He had wrecked the yacht, put her up on the beach and knocked Ted out, but it was Aria who was ultimately responsible for *Pssst!* and her crew. He wished he could think clearly, but his mind seemed to have clogged.

Aria abandoned her dinghy and ran. Fine sand spurted up behind her feet. "Oscar! Oscar!" she yelled, "Oscar, are you alright?" She stumbled as a shell cut the side of her foot but she kept running. "Oscar!"

Chapter Twenty-three

Tap … taptap. Aria opened her eyes to see a palm frond roof. She had been deeply asleep, sprawled on a low bunk, the only furniture in the room, with a mosquito coil burning its last some distance away on a little metal frame on the sand. It was early morning and the first light showed through the woven walls and door. Her foot throbbed gently under a bandage stained with Friar's Balsam.

Tap … taptap. Aria had been brought here at dusk, told she could sleep and would be taken to Suva next day. Oscar was left securing *Pssst!*, with the man she had met on the beach giving instructions. He'd taken Aria's sevusevu, waved her into an outrigger canoe and a couple of amused Fijians had brought her here at high speed. They laughed together and occasionally, their grins even broader, gave her a thumbs-up. She had been hungry, but there was nothing to do but lie down and sleep.

"Oscar? Is that you?" she whispered now.

His low-pitched laugher sounded just through the woven partition. "Yeah, I'm in the palm frond jail too, Aria. I think it's part of the chief's house. The guest annex. I thought you were there because I heard you talking in your sleep."

"Oh! Um … what did I say?"

"It sounded like, 'I will show proof to the country', in your bossy lawyer's voice. 'Contrary', I guess."

Aria laughed; she was glad that was all she'd said. "I'm already arguing it in my sleep. When did they bring you here? I guessed you'd be somewhere in custody, and I think this is custody."

There was a low chuckle. "Yeah, it is. This place is cute—not what you'd call secure custody. We could just walk out of here."

"Don't you even think about it. We are in enough trouble already without ..."

"It's okay. I won't. I was just thinking what a nice friendly jail it is, for my first one."

"We're on an island, Oscar. The island is the real jail. You'd be going nowhere. We need to be co-operative and sensible, and trust that the right process has started. I just wish I knew what's happened to Bree. But if she was here, she'd know about this. At least they have Ted. And the dope. We're lucky, really, when you think about it."

Oscar seemed to be able to do nothing but laugh. "Yep, I feel lucky. Coulda got shot, coulda got hijacked, coulda done my next voyage with a deranged drug-runner. Could be in a real jail. Pretty lucky. I suppose we'll be here for a while, will we? How's it go, lawyer lady?"

"Ohh ... Fijian criminal law, I'd suppose. Maybe crossed with marine law crossed with international law ... none of those my thing. Maybe it will turn out to be *sui generis*; that would be exciting."

"What does that mean?"

"In a class of its own—unique. It won't be, though." Aria laughed. "We'll just take it as it comes. Marine law is comprehensive but pretty unguessable. If I get the one call that they get in the movies, I'll ring Bettison. He'll help deal with it and he has an old colleague or two up here, I think, from his student days. He'd know who to have represent us. Hey, Oscar, what happened after the chief came and they took me away?"

"Not a lot. I secured *Pssst!* as best I could after Ted had been lifted off and put on the fishing boat for Levuka—it came back. Jeez, I hope that guy is alright! He was out for a long time. Came to as they were putting him in the fishing boat, but he didn't do anything, just looked around and lolled back. I think I hit him *much* too hard. Never hit anyone before. That's the thing I'm most worried about."

"Well, we'll find out in time, so don't agonise over it. Wait 'til you know and meantime, envisage a positive outcome. What happened with the drugs or whatever it was? Awkward for them here."

"They set a guard. They waited while I did all sorts of jobs. The chief sent off for a couple of people from … well, I don't know where, maybe the clam farm. I used some glue stuff from the bosun's locker to fill the bullet hole. Didn't have to touch anything to get it out. There were a couple of tubes in those top drawers that were exposed. It might have let water in, though somehow *Pssst!* seems to be a fair ol' way up the beach. The smashed bit is well forward. Maybe the tide went out, I dunno." The bed rustled as Oscar rolled over. "Anyway, I screwed all the hatches down hard as I could, though one was distorted and not closing too well. They helped me check a few things like whether any fuel was leaking—nothing, as far as I could tell. Then the chief guy collected our passports and locked up. He has them, the keys and our wallets and a few bits. I'm glad Harky whittled another mermaid so it wasn't that embarrassing thing Ted had. They've set a local guy as guard on the boat, holding Ted's gun. They were a bit short of guns. Haha!

Anyway, that's any fingerprints gone. Oh … there would have been mine too, so good thing they're gone."

"Yep, that might be fortunate. But you'll need to tell the exact truth anyway. Admit you grabbed the gun from him. Well, let's see what happens. They'll take us back to Suva soon, I think, and deal with it all there. I don't know how they'll get *Pssst!* off. That's a fair bit of reef you threw her over. But I think they rescue yachts all the time here—it's a Fijian specialty. Pity; she was a lovely yacht." Aria's voice was wistful.

Oscar gave a soft laugh. "I really hope she's not munted; she doesn't look too good. I still thought I might work on her, provided Ted didn't make an appearance too often. But Ted won't be chartering now. Perhaps he never intended to. Or perhaps chartering was going to be his means of distribution, under cover of guests. Who knows, eh. You were right about him, Aria, dead dodgy."

"Dodgy but … haha … let's not mention dead. You know, I am convinced Bree's bloke Manny knew something. I wonder if they were in it together? He was too interested in that boat. I thought it strange at the time, but I looked around her very carefully and found nothing and decided it was just Manny being Mannyish. I don't know … there was a concatenation of clues … "

"Jeez, Aria, a whaat?"

"… a pile-up … a stringing together of clues. But I couldn't make anything of them. That was because I was looking for something, instead of looking for what *couldn't* be seen. Different approach." She was silent for a moment. "Maybe Manny thought Ted was double-crossing or cheating him. It all just adds to my worries about Bree, though. She's linked to both of them."

"But Aria, it'll be like my GBH. You just have to wait and see, now."

"GBH! Come on, I don't think they'll charge you with that. I don't know if they even have GBH. Fijians are famous for fighting—in New Zealand anyway. It might be no big deal. And noone's going to believe Ted. They'll find out about the construction of the boat in Thailand, they'll follow the whole trail. I think the stuff must have come already packed aboard in Thailand. Cunning construction."

Oscar sighed. "Yeah. We missed it. And Suva customs missed it. I suppose it means we're no dumber than the rest. You know I think Ted was clever. He waited a long time, picked you because you're the gal least likely and are a skilled sailor, irked you so you'd keep your distance and I'd get pissed off with him, got close to Bree as a weapon to use against you if he needed one. He managed it pretty well. But obviously, customs here had heard something. They were suspicious, so maybe they'd been tipped off, but didn't find it. Ted would have set up a very lucrative business. He's clever, alright. Is he clever enough to pin it on us?"

"No. It was in a purpose-built compartment. He's guilty, *ab initio*."

There was a sound of movement outside and Oscar's door opened. A silent Fijian beckoned to him and signed to get Aria. "Aria, we're being taken out. Hope it's breakfast. I'm crazy hungry." Neither had eaten since the morning before.

"I'm hungry too but it had better be the loo first." Aria jumped up and winced. She rolled the side of her foot up. By the look of the Friar's Balsam patch on the bandage, it was only a small cut. She wondered when she had last put on clean clothes but she had nothing with her.

The door was fastened with a loop of coir string. Outside, Aria found Oscar with the chief and a big tough looking fellow who spoke English. She asked to wash and was directed to an outside long-drop with a tank nearby and high tap. Washing was a huge relief but, feeling somewhat guilty because the water had to be collected on a roof, she let it pour over her like the monsoon for only a minute. She joined Oscar, smiling and dragging her fingers through her dripping hair to untangle it.

He murmured, "You're beautiful with wet hair," and it made her almost dizzy. But perhaps I'm famished, she thought.

***

Back in Suva, the streets steamed. Aria and Oscar were not immediately under arrest but could not leave Suva until a Magistrate's hearing took place when any charges would be formally laid. The phrases made Oscar's heart sink, but Aria took it all in her stride.

Outside, she sent a message to Carlotta. Carlotta called immediately. "Aria! You were quick! But I know why. Bree wasn't there. Hey, I got good news for you. I had a ... you whaaaat? Fanny! Are you kidding? Oh, my! ... Ted had? And Oscar ... *hah*! *That boy*! Hey I'm running down the steps right now—I'm coming. Yep, the Police headquarters. Be there soon."

Carlotta arrived in a taxi. "Aria! Oscar! At least you're safe and okay." She hugged them both.

"Lotta, how's everything? How's Harky?" When Carlotta nodded, Aria went on. "We need to clean up—we've been in these clothes for days. Well, nearly three. Of course, we now have no other clothes. Oh, and nor do you!"

Carlotta directed them to the little lodge she had found through hospital staff. "I'll go right away and buy two T shirts and pants and bring them to the lodge. And undies! Stand under the shower 'til I get there."

They had to tell the police where they would be. Carlotta was amused. "You're lucky you weren't *given* accommodation! Secure. Listen, Aria, I got hold of Bree. She's fine—she's not in Fiji at all. Ted lied. She's back in Auckland and Manny Freidman has left New Zealand and … well—she's quite ok. You call her; she'll explain it all herself."

"Bree? At home? Oh! I'll call her! I can't imagine … Oscar, would you go to this place and get two rooms? No, I'd better come and shower and then I can call Bree."

"Hey, don't get your hopes up about this place. You don't get a room. It's dorms really—a women's room and a men's one. There's only me in the women's." She made big eyes. "I ain't checked the men's."

"It'll be fine. Last night was a bit different too, but we slept. Hey Lotta, how is Harky?"

Carlotta shook her head of grey curls. "The same, my poor old darlin'. They've moved him to a step down unit. They're pretty sure it's brain stem as well and are gonna fly him to Auckland. I'll go too. He's in worse trouble than you guys, I reckon."

"Oh Lotta, I hope there's good news soon. Just drop the clothes and we'll meet up at the hospital; we haven't seen Harky since the rescue. We'll visit him."

"You can't. They won't let you in, where he is. Infection control stuff. Let's eat somewhere but you'll surely have to avoid the yacht club—you'll be the subject of every conversation and the story gettin' bigger every minute. Those yachties' VHF scheds, they're like news channel real-time." She made her eyes big and wobbled her head.

They left the police station and Aria stopped in a little shop for more phone credit. "Oh Oscar! Bree in New Zealand and okay! I hope that means not actively involved. Except she'll be linked by association."

After her shower, squeezed into the T shirt and jeans that Carlotta had thrown over the shower door, Aria walked down to the waterfront and leaned on a palm trunk. "Bree, it's Aria. Oh Bree, I've been *so* worried."

"Arz! So worried? Why? Cos I didn't call for three days? That's not like you. You'd easily go three days without ringing *me*. No, seriously, I did appreciate hearing from you when you were at sea but I knew as soon as you got to Suva … hey, how is Harky?"

"No better; they think it's also brainstem so they're flying him home. Bree, we didn't know what had happened to you. Ted said you were on Makogai, waiting for me, and I thought … well I don't know what I thought." Aria turned and saw Oscar sitting on a seat in the shade of a palm tree with a young Fijian policewoman.

"Ted said I was in Fiji? That's crazy! He knew where I was. He gave Manny and me a few days at a resort near Opua. He had a booking he couldn't cancel 'cos it was already paid for, so he gave it to Manny and we had three days there. No internet, no mobile coverage. It's a sort of a retreat, really. I couldn't ring you but I didn't think you'd worry."

Aria listened with surprise. "So you … you had no idea about Ted and *Pssst!* and … Bree, listen, you might be in trouble having accepted a gift from Ted, and being associated with him. He had drugs aboard *Pssst!*, probably ever since Thailand, and we found them and … oh, it's a … a long story, but Oscar and I, well, we're in trouble here. I'll keep you posted. You'll be under suspicion, too. Now *listen*! Don't tell any lies if you're questioned. Tell the truth and tell it all." There was silence for a few moments and she went on, "The truth is important."

"Oh Arz!"

"I'll tell you about it when I can, and meantime, don't worry. I think we'll be OK, really. But if the police ask you anything, Bree, tell the truth. That's the important thing."

"Okaaay, but it's a bit awkward. About Manny, Arz. I'm not supposed to know. I hacked—well I didn't *hack*, exactly—I *looked at* his computer. There was always so much I didn't know about Manny."

"Yep, so much no one knew."

"I knew he'd never been in Australia for more than a few weeks but he had an Australian passport. I never knew where he really came from or much about his family, you know? He was so secretive and always disappearing and reappearing. It was awful really." She made some sound, a sigh, perhaps, but it could have been a sob. "Well, he told me that last morning at the resort he was going away—permanently. He said he wouldn't be able to keep in touch, but he wouldn't say why. That's just how it is, he said, and I'd better forget him. So when he got a stomach upset from breakfast and was throwing up for ages, I looked at his computer." Bree's voice took on a defensive tone. "He wouldn't say *where* he was going, either, Arz. I … I just wanted to *know* things, and he'd left his computer on when he started vomiting. He was sooo sick." Her breath was ragged. "Parts of it needed passwords and a lot was in other languages and some in a blocky script, Hebrew maybe, some in an Arabic script and an Asian one, but from what I *could* read, I'm guessing he was an agent and something to do with tracking drug rings. It was all too weird for words. I think he was on a false passport, Arz, I think he was really—well, I don't know. Bloody Manny! He strung me along for all this time. I feel so stupid. And he even spied on my work, I realise now. He used to come when I worked overtime and look at stuff and ask questions. He wasn't honest with me, ever." She made another odd noise.

Aria felt tempted to say, "Well, surprise, surprise," but resisted because Bree sounded so hurt. "Bree, move on. Don't even bother to find out the truth. Just let the whole thing go. If Manny was doing a job, he's done it, I'd assume. It sounds as if he wasn't involved; probably knew something but not enough, or investigating, as you said. But it's over." She heard a little murmur of assent. "Bree, I'll keep in touch. I don't know what's happening yet, but at present we just have to stay in Suva and be available. Ted … well, I don't know where Ted is; probably been arrested, or maybe he's in hospital—he got, um—injured." Was that a reasonable way of putting it? "I hope we'll be back soon, but there's an awful lot of sorting out to be done. I'll call my office and explain. I might need their help. But just at present, there's nothing to do. Hey Bree, I'll go before my new credit's out. I'll call again. Keep this number, eh?"

"Yep, bye Arz. Thanks. For calling. And for all that advice on Manny over the years." Aria heard a laugh with a catch in it and Bree murmured, "Arz? I love you, Arz" and the call dropped.

She called her office. George Bettison laughed when he heard her voice. "Tell me." He grunted through her explanation, clearly knowing something about it already. "I'll sort a defence for you. Young Isiah is insisting he come up. Seems to think knowing the ropes up there in the Islands is the main thing. Hah! But don't worry, Aria, there are others I can put you in touch with. I'll be in contact."

The young policewoman finished telling Oscar where to get real Fijian food and said goodbye.

"I don't think she's going too far. She just *happened* along, started chatting and *happened* to know where you were." Oscar laughed. "But she did have some stuff to tell us."

"Ah, not under arrest but being tailed."

"Maybe. But she did have a purpose in finding us. She gave me these." He waved some papers. "There'll be a hearing in the Magistrate's Court tomorrow, and we have to be there. And Ted! Ted's going to be there too. That's what this says." Oscar folded the papers messily and stuffed them into his pocket. "It means he's on his feet."

Chapter Twenty-four

The Magistrate's Court was a spartan affair, with a minimum of furniture and a Fiji coat of arms behind the Magistrate's desk. Aria had never presented herself in court in anything but the most formal clothes and now felt embarrassed. I look like a total scruff, she thought. Here I am in court, in a T shirt and jeans—tight ones at that. But then the clothes I had aboard Pssst! were no smarter, just my size.

Much of the proceedings was in Fijian and the court seemed full of tall officials in tailored sulus. Aria and Oscar recognised some of them and got nods from the customs men and the officer from Biosecurity. English was used when Aria and Oscar had to identify themselves. Both were shocked when Ted was brought in, handcuffed to a policeman. The once dapper man looked as if he had slept rough, his face puffy and stubbled, and he took care not to meet their eyes.

The police had most of the say and it was alarming for Aria and Oscar to hear their names but not know what was being said. At one point, the Magistrate, with his eyes down on the notes he was taking, gave a 'Humph!" and smiled. Finally, the Magistrate addressed the court, first in Fijian, then briefly in English. "It seems that Captain Stihl and Mr Niu have no case to answer. Mr Thadeus Phillipe Halaby is charged with possession of a Class A drug, with importation to Fiji of a Class A drug, with failing to …" It went on.

Oscar sneaked his hand across and squeezed Aria's. Her face was impassive, but he knew by her stillness that she was nervous.

The Magistrate looked down at his papers. "Captain Stihl and Mr Niu are required to attend the hearing of these cases as witnesses for the Crown, on a date or dates to be set and if leaving the country for any reason, must pay a bond …" Aria gave the slightest of nods.

When it was over, the magistrate left and a hubbub broke out. They made their way towards the door and as they did, Oscar glimpsed Manny across the room. He grabbed Aria's arm. "Aria!" he whispered, "Manny's here, Manny Friedmann! Over to our left, with the police and customs guys."

Aria stretched her neck in time to see Manny, looking very different in a suit, leaving through the door the Magistrate had taken. One of the court officials had his hand on Manny's shoulder, and was bending to talk to him. The blood surged to her face with annoyance. "So he *did* know something! He could have warned us off Ted. Could have saved us this mess if he'd been any good at his job."

Oscar shook his head. "It wasn't his job to look after us, Aria. Bree was prob'ly right; he's an agent and maybe it's something bigger than just this case."

Outside, they turned towards the harbour. Aria's mood lifted. "Well. No GBH." She laughed. She could see Carlotta waiting for them.

Oscar was grinning. "I'm relieved Ted's alright. I wanted to stop him, not hurt him. And I'd be a gonner if he'd been seriously injured or carked it. So I was pleased to see him, for once. You know, I thought you'd be charged with *something* … negligence as Captain, maybe, and I'd get at least assault, wilful damage to property … a list, just not half as long as Ted's. Ted got the book!"

Carlotta rushed up to them. "Aria! Oscar! What's happening?"

Aria hugged her. She was hot and sweaty, and Aria got a wet cheek. "Well, to our surprise, we're not charged with anything: just have to appear as witnesses, which I'll be glad to do. We have to wait to hear when the case will be tried to find out if we go home or not first. But we'd have to pay a bond and I rather think it would be hefty. So I'm hoping it's soon and we stay. I *really* want my sat phone back—and my hand bearing compass and our other stuff."

"Fanny! I can't wait to tell Harky this."

"Tell Harky? Is he conscious?"

"No. Well, doesn't seem to be. But you never know what the unresponsive hear and understand. So I've been tellin' him the story—I whisper it to him; *sub judicae*, huh?"

Aria laughed. "Yep, it probably is. Oh, I do hope he can understand and enjoy it."

They bought coconut water, and sat sipping. Oscar looked at Carlotta's face. She had lost weight in the short time since Harky's stroke—not even two weeks. "Let's hope he recovers, eh. He's a remarkable guy, old Harky. You're lucky, Carlotta."

"Oh, Harky's great, Oscar, sure. But he was never … you know … the one for me, really. We're just very dear friends. He'll love his wife forever, and for me, there'll never be anyone after Aria's dad."

Aria looked up. "Oh!" She gazed at Carlotta, trying to remember her father and Carlotta together, things they said, clues. She couldn't think of a lot. Dad had just been Dad. "I didn't know … oh, Lotta, that's tragic."

"No, it's not, Princess. We had all those wonderful years, and the way it was, that suited us just fine. I'm cool with it. There'll just never be another Tom."

***

Harky was airlifted out to Auckland next day. Carlotta flew with him. She stood holding Aria's arm, watching him being lifted by stretcher out of an ambulance. "I'll see you there, Princess. Fanny! This has been a marathon. Keep me posted, huh? I gotta keep that guy amused. See ya, world's best."

Oscar and Aria took a boat out to a resort on Kadavu Island. It was a busy place, so they scrambled over rocks and through dense bush until they reached a little beach. Aria threw herself down on the pinkish sand. "Oh, that's what I need for the moment. Blot out the civilised world."

Oscar peeled off his T shirt and shorts. "You coming in? I can't wait. All that ocean for two weeks and no swimming. It's been like smelling hot bread when the shop's closed."

It was the first time Aria had seen his tattooed body close. She thought it exquisite—hot bread, indeed, and the shop must stay closed. She carefully put the thought aside. "You go in. Swimming's not my thing, with my wardrobe difficulties."

Oscar shrugged. "No problem to me; up to you. Don't roast, whitey. Even in the shade, it's pretty sunny, eh." He sprinted down the beach and into the water. She watched him swimming up and down close in, occasionally diving down and popping up, at ease in the water. He came out, water spilling off his body and threw himself down beside her.

She sat up. He turned and put a wet arm around her. She wanted the moment to last forever but she pushed back from him. "Oscar, you mustn't hope for anything for us. It can't be. You … I'll end up spoiling your life. There's … well, there's things that might not work out …"

He kept his arm across her shoulders, his face close to hers. "Let's see, eh? I'm just happy to be with you and I still want to see you when we get back to Auckland. Yes? I can? When we both get back to work—or not?"

She shook her head but whispered, "Yes."

He laughed. "Alright. It can be your call, eh." He dropped his arm. "And I won't let it mess me up."

She gave a sad little smile. "You might not be able to prevent it."

Oscar lay back, still smiling, his eyes closed. Aria looked down at his face—how perfect it was—and watched him breathe. "Oh, I forgot to tell you—I called Bettison again this morning. He'd been in touch with his friend up here, who's still a practising barrister. He was going to take our case or cases, if we needed defence. Isiah Macdonald—do you know him? Isiah works with me—he's from Espiritu. Well, he was ready to fly up, too. I doubt he would have been useful, really; Fiji law would likely be different from Vanuatu law. But Bettison says it's fine; he'll stand the bond and we should just come home. He'll *send* us back to get his bond. Haha!" She lay back on the sand by Oscar's shoulder.

His grin spread over his face. "Bettison's paying *my* bond too? We are pretty lucky alright. Might take me a while to settle down, after this is finished, but you know, I want to quit work and keep sailing. What about you?"

Aria turned to peer at him, her eyes crinkled. "You think anyone would take you on? You just wrecked your last yacht on a reef. Your career as a sailor is burnt toast."

"Well, I didn't do it because of incompetence or carelessness, Aria. I *put* her there." His eyes crinkled. "I careened her."

"Hah! *Put* her over the coral and onto the beach, a bit smashed up! Actually, it's fine for you. You're lauded in the New Zealand papers, apparently—the brave hero who disarmed the crim and brought him to justice. I come out as a pretty dumb lawyer. We're supposed to be good at smelling rats, us lawyers. I'm not looking my best in the press."

"You're looking pretty good to me."

She smiled. "Oscar, there's something I want to know. Why did you put *two* plans into action?" Aria could not keep the amusement out of her voice. "Putting the yacht on the beach *and* laying Ted out?"

Oscar sat up and turned towards her. "I didn't. I only followed one plan—beaching Ted's yacht so he couldn't force me to sail him somewhere. I didn't *plan* to jump him—I just saw the chance and did it." He gazed out over the sparkling sea, a huge grin creasing his face. "But yeah, maybe somewhere in the back of my mind, I realised there was a big fault in plan A and I needed a quick B. Well, that's how it goes with plans."

Aria laughed and sat up beside him, her voice as warm as the sand she brushed off his back. "We'll need new plans. I've still got an old one, but I like your idea of having a few. And maybe some together."

Oscar smiled, his dark eyes on her. "*And pluck 'til time and times are done/ The silver apples of the moon/ The golden apples of the sun.*"

The End

until …

... more about Aria in *The Roar of the Silent Sea*

The Roar of the Silent Sea

Aria achieves her dream of a single-handed ocean passage on *Trinkitat*, her beloved little nine-metre yacht, yet events spiral out of control again. She has arranged to meet Oscar and Bree in Vanuatu but twin cyclones ravage the islands ...

Then on her return voyage, she has an accident. Alone, she must use her wits and endurance to survive. By the time she completes her home voyage, she finds the courage to embrace an unforeseen future.

Sailing Terms

Abate: reduce, usually used to refer to reduction in wind strength or wave height:

Abeam: opposite the middle of the ship, or on a line at right angles to the vessel

Aft: anything further back than half the length, or behind the main mast

Aloft: above, up the mast or into the rigging of a ship

Amidships: in the middle of a vessel, most often laterally but possibly longitudinally

Astern: behind or towards the rear

Athwart: across from side to side

Back (of wind direction): to change in a clockwise direction

Back or aback (of sails): to catch the wind on the wrong side

Back- or forestays: wires that support the mast

Baggywrinkle: frayed rope knotted together and tied round the standing rigging to prevent chafe

Beam: the widest part of the vessel, 'on the beam': 90 degrees to the vessel's heading

Bear off: to increase the angle of the vessel to the wind

Beaufort Scale: measure of wind strength related to observed conditions at sea (or on land)

Before: in front of the main mast

Belay: secure a line/sheet/halyard usually with a figure of eight on a cleat or bollard

Below: below deck, the interior of a vessel

Boat hook: pole with a hook and spike used to fend off or pull

Boom: horizontal spar to which the foot of a sail is attached

Bosun's locker: where maintenance gear is stored

Bow(s): the front of a vessel

Carling: internal support work of either the deck or hatches

Careened: positioned on the side, usually out of water

Coaming: raised border of the cockpit or hatch to keep out water

Cockpit: open well in the deck outside any deckhouse or cabin, containing steering and controls

Col: area between two weather systems, often associated with neutral conditions

Clew (see tack and head): on a triangular sail, the point of attachment of the sheet

Clouds: Low: cumulus, stratus, cumulo-nimbus and strato-cumulus Mid-height: alto-cumulus, alto-stratus and nimbo-stratus High: cirrus, cirro-stratus and cirro-cumulus

Cutter rigged ketch: vessel having two headsails on forestays, a main sail and a mizzen sail

Danforth anchor: anchor having two triangular blades set at an acute angle to the shank

Direction (of wind): the compass point from which the wind is *coming*

Direction (of water current): the compass point to which the flow is *going*

Dodger: short for spray dodger; a structure to shelter the cockpit or helmsman

EPIRB: emergency position indicating radio beacon

Finger: long floating pontoon in a marina

Flake down: bring down the mainsail in folds so it can be lashed onto the boom

Forecastle (pron. fo'c'sle): the forward cabin

Forward (pron. forred): towards the bow

Genoa: large headsail

Gunwales (pron. gunnels): upper edge of the topsides

Halyard: line used to hoist a sail

Helm: the device (tiller or wheel) by which a ship is steered by hand

Ketch: two masted vessel with mizzen forward of the rudder post & shorter than the main mast

Leach and luff: the aft and forward edges respectively of a sail

Mast: tall spar on the centre line of a vessel, to support a sail

Mainsail: large triangular sail raised on the main mast and footed by the main boom

Mayday: radio telecommunication to indicate a life-threatening emergency

Mizzen: shorter aft mast with its own boom

Painter: line for securing a dinghy or tender

Pan: (pan-pan) radio telecommunication to indicate a non-life-threatening emergency.

Port (also see starboard): left, facing forward

Quarter: an aft quadrant of a vessel, 45 degrees aft of abeam

Rake: slight backward angle of the mast

Ratlines (pron. ratlins): thin lines between the close shrouds allowing easy climbing aloft

Reaching: sailing across the wind, from about 60 degrees to 160 degrees

Reef: bar of rock, coral or sand beneath the water

Reef (a sail): reduce the working area of a sail by lowering and lashing down or furling

RHIB: rigid hull inflatable boat

Rope: line attached to a bucket; all others lines are called a sheet, halyard, shroud, stay, painter, vang, or lift

Scuppers: holes under the toe rail to allow water to flow off the deck

Sheet: line attached to the clew of a sail to control and set the sail

Shrouds: part of standing rigging; lateral support for a mast, now usually stainless steel

Spinnaker: large light sail with a free luff set forward of the mast when running downwind

Spreaders: horizontal bars on the mast which redirect the supporting force of the shrouds

Starboard (pron. starb'ed): right, facing forward. Port and starboard never change.

Staysail: small triangular stabilising sail rigged forward of the main mast

Stiff: having a large righting lever and tending not to incline or roll much

Tender (adj): having a small righting lever at any angle and therefore tending to roll

Tender (n): dinghy; small boat used to go to and fro when anchored off

Vang: line attached to the boom to prevent it lifting or the sail backing

Veer (wind direction): change in a counterclockwise direction

Yankee jib: high cut foresail which does not take water in a rough sea

New Zealand Terms

Bro: brother, friend

Bugger: not offensive, usually a substitute for Mate, Bro

Cark it: die

Dodgy: not trustworthy or not correct

GBH: short for 'grievous bodily harm'

Godzone: 'God's own country', New Zealand

Munted: broken, usually meaning broken beyond repair

'Naki (usually <u>the</u> 'Naki): Taranaki, province in North Island

Ropeable: very angry, hinting restraint may be required

Sweet: good

Too much: an expression of appreciation or admiration

Uce: Samoan equivalent of bro or sis (pronounced oo-ss), with strict rules of usage

Wops: remote or rural area

Yob: badly behaved or uncultured person

About the Author

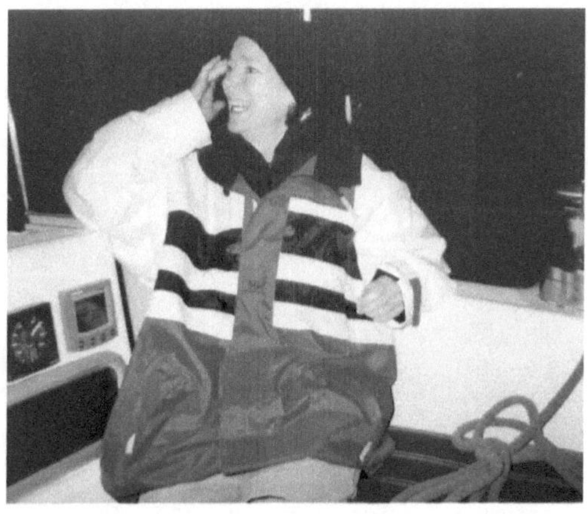

Anne Millen was born in central Queensland and educated at the Comet State School, the Primary Correspondence School, Rockhampton Girls' Grammar School and University of Queensland. She qualified as a physiotherapist aged twenty and a year later, went to New Zealand as an existential migrant. She married a keen sailor in Wellington, and spent a decade raising two children before sailing round the world with them on *Rehuata*. Later she lived in Oman for three years, remarried, and moved to Abu Dhabi and then Dubai. She worked as a physiotherapist, editing the *Gazelle* and writing short stories and newspaper articles. She retired to Sri Lanka where she spent four happy years. She now lives between Australia and New Zealand. She is a vagabond and a slow writer.

Contact: **annemillenauthor@gmail.com**

Website: **annemillenauthor.com**